The Art of Falling in Love with Your Best Friend

ANNE KEMP

To James William AKA 'Dubs'
my partner in crime
(You really ARE the best driver in the family! Don't tell anyone.
Ever!)

I've been a paramedic for a couple of years now, and I know that not all of my calls are going to go as perfectly as we want them to or the way our classrooms prepare us for. I had to face the fact that my "I am woman, hear me roar" work mantra may need adjusting in some instances, because I may need to pivot in my thinking.

Now, don't get me wrong, we are trained for anything that could potentially come flying our way in any given situation because the world is full of surprises these days.

Surprises like the time someone tried to wrestle a fox and was subsequently worried they could have rabies, so they needed us on the scene and pronto. Another time, someone was sent a "glitter bomb" which can be soooo delightful—yes, if you think you detect sarcasm there, you are correct. A glitter bomb is a package that shoots out nothing but glitter when it's opened. When this one was opened, the receivers accidentally inhaled the contents, as did a few family members who were over that night to celebrate our victim-patient's birthday. Fun times.

So for us paramedics, it's not hard to tell when someone is

genuinely frightened, and looking at this dear elderly woman wrapped in her fluffy green nightgown in front of me, I'm for sure feeling the frightened vibe. Ever since we arrived on the scene at her home a few moments ago, she hasn't appeared to be in pain, just scared.

I do a quick visual assessment, looking for anything that could stand out, but don't see any signs of harm or injury. Stepping forward, I gently place a hand on her shoulder. "What's your name?"

She keeps her eyes trained on the ceiling, twitching as she takes a few steps back. "Carol."

Exchanging a look with my ambulance partner and best friend, Reid, he inclines his head toward the interior of the home. It's his silent way of telling me he's going to walk around and check things out.

Watching him go, I turn my attention back to Carol. "Is there anyone else in the house with you?"

Life would be easier, and so would the job, if people would tell us what's wrong, but sometimes we have to coerce it out of them. I watch as Carol lowers herself to sit on the floor. Figuring I'm in it for the long haul at this point, I slide onto the floor to sit beside Carol.

I'm fidgety by nature, so staying still on the floor with her begins to kick in my own anxious need to move around. Using my thumb, I feel around my ring finger, finding the Christmas gift Reid gave me last year—a fidget spinner ring. The tiny band is threaded through six small silver balls, and all six of them soothe me as I touch them slowly, using each rotation of each tiny orb to bring calm.

As my own version of fight or flight stalls out, I lean over so Carol can see into my eyes. "Did something upset you? We're here to help, so let us help you, okay?"

As the words fall out of my mouth, a screeching sound pierces the air with some kind of flying bundle dive-bombing my head and causing a breeze of air around me. Out of instinct I duck, swatting an arm in the air as Carol throws herself into my chest.

"Get that thing out of here!" Her half yell, half caterwaul hits my ear, its pitch discombobulating me for a moment. Glancing up, I look around for Reid to see if he can offer any advice for what to do next, but I quickly realize he's discovered her issue.

"Look." He points to the ceiling of the living room, his hand tracking the movement of something suspended above us. Squinting, I look where he points, but the light in this room is too dim. I jump to my feet and head for a switch on the wall so I can get a better look at the room and the situation.

Shouldn't have done that.

After flipping the switch, I turn around, keeping my eyes trained on the ceiling and looking for whatever this thing is that's in this woman's home. This is the moment said creature again dive-bombs my head, screeching and crying, sounding like a dozen mice squeaking but at a higher frequency. Something flapping hits my hair, tugging on it hard enough that my head is pulled along with it, but for some reason it thankfully lets go of my tresses. Serves me right for not tying it back in a ponytail tonight.

"What is that?" I scream while backing up flat against the wall.

"I think it's a bat," Carol whispers from her position, which is now under the console table.

"That's what we consider the headline, Carol," Reid teases as he sights the bat and follows it around the living room. "Next time, lead with that so we know what we're walking into."

"It came out of nowhere! I arrived home and was about to close the windows and go to bed when that thing appeared in here." She moans a little as she pulls her robe tighter around her tiny frame. "Circling the room and trying to land in my hair. Disgusting creatures."

Thinking back to the hair pull I experienced a few minutes ago, I wonder if we're dealing with a bat with a hair fetish. I start to make a joke about it, but seeing the worry still etched on Carol's face, I change my mind. Anyway, Reid's usually the one who cracks a joke when it's unnecessary, not me.

"Okay, one thing I know about bats is that light can disorient them sometimes." I flip the switch off for the over-head light, leaving only the dimly lit lamp in the far corner of the room. "Reid, I'm going to leave the front door open, but let's also open some windows to give this guy a chance to get out."

Reid is already across the room and throwing windows open. "Good thing it's summertime, Carol. If this had been winter, we'd be freezing."

"If this had been winter, I'd be in Florida," Carol grumbles. So much for seeing the bright side.

Peering around the room, I spot a large bowl full of popcorn next to a stack of magazines. In a few quick strides, I cross the room to grab the bowl and the sturdiest magazine of the bunch.

"Really? Need a five-minute break real quick, Dylan?" Reid cuts his eyes my way, teasing.

"Har har." I tip the bowl outside one of the open windows. "Sorry, Carol, I owe you some popcorn."

She peeks out from under her hiding spot. "I can't have salt. So if you do replace it, unsalted, okay?"

"Noted." Chewing my cheek to keep from laughing, I turn my attention back to the ceiling and to Reid. "Where is it?"

Reid spins in a circle, looking around the room. It's not a large room, but big enough. The ceilings are high and the curtains around the windows are made of thick material. Lots of dark crevices for a bat to park himself.

I make my way into the middle of the room, trying to keep my wits about me. Anytime we're out on a call, the adrenaline always kicks in, but my Spidey senses are on a super high-alert status after having this stray bat personally attack my hair.

"There."

I turn to look where Reid's pointing. He's found the little sucker, hanging upside-down on an old wrought-iron curtain rod. We don't have time to get a ladder for me to climb up so I can reach him, but there is an overstuffed chair nearby. Judging from the width of its arms, I should be able to balance myself on it and capture this guy.

I get Reid's attention and hold up the items in my hands.

"Can you spot me?" I nod toward the chair. "I'll get up there and trap him in this bowl, then slide the magazine over the top to keep him safe until we get him outside, okay?"

"Sexist." Reid's serious when he looks at me, his eyes brown as polished amber.

I meet his gaze for a second, but quickly turn around and make my way over to the chair and start climbing onto it. He follows suit; I know this because in a matter of moments I feel his strong hands on my back and legs supporting me. I hand him the magazine to hold while I secure the bowl in both of my hands.

"What are you talking about, sexist?"

"You're calling the bat 'he' like you know it's a guy." Reid's hand tightens around my waist as he stabilizes my lower half. "Are you saying that because he's lost and won't ask for help?"

"Shush," I manage through gritted teeth––don't tell him, but I love it when we banter like this. "Life is short, and I can't handle your humor right now. Not when this bat could jump out and eat my face."

"You should be wearing your gloves," Reid reminds me, swallowing a laugh.

"I should be, but we're here now." Stretching myself to full length, I'm almost able to reach the bat, but not quite there. "I need to lean forward a little more."

"No way." Reid's grip tightens even more around my waist, his fingers adding pressure as he presses them into my sides. "We'll need a ladder if you need to stretch more. It's too risky. I can't hold you."

I am so close, I swear I can see the bat smiling at me. I decide to try another inch, so I stretch a little more, kind of in awe of the fact that this thing isn't moving at all. I've seen this done on some wildlife show or a random YouTube video my dad watched once, where a guy had a bat fly into his house. All he had to do to get it out was cover it with a bowl, slide something over the top of it as a temporary lid, and voilà...the bat was outta the house.

Eyes on the prize, I lean forward a touch more. "Just stay here, Reid, and don't let go of me."

My support system grunts. "You're going to pull us both over the chair if you keep trying, Dylan. Come down and let's just leave the doors and windows open to this room and let it leave on its own."

"No way." I start to shake my head, then think twice about it. Do not need to wave my hair in front of this thing again and get his attention. I'm centimeters, at this point, away from encasing the little guy in the bowl. "I've...almost...got...him."

There's a groan, and I feel something pinching my side. "I can't hold on to you like this, Dylan, my fingers are...WAIT!"

I'm really not sure what flipped me out more—the fact the bat chose the moment I was closing in to push off from his spot and launch himself at my face, or the fact that Reid started to lose his grasp on me and I could feel myself falling, weightless and without limits, tumbling backward and throwing the plastic popcorn bowl into the air and over my head.

Lucky for me, there's an oversized couch next to the chair. As I hit its cushions, I twist around, looking for the bat only to watch in horror as Reid comes toppling down on top of me. His weight strikes me in the chest at full force, knocking the wind out of me and splaying my legs wide open.

I take a series of calming breaths before opening my eyes to find Reid smiling down at me. His breath hits my cheek and his eyes are for real twinkling. I know this guy, and he's trying really hard right now not to laugh at me, and all I can do is think about the fact I can essentially taste his breath right now. Grape bubble gum, I'm pretty sure.

"Very strategic of you, my dear. We showed that bat what's what, didn't we?"

"Shut up." I try to sit up, but can't do it with Reid sprawled on top of me. I push on his shoulders a little. "Get outta my way, we need to get that bat."

"Did you say you got the bat?" Carol's voice squeaks from her spot under the table.

"Not yet, but we're close." I hate lying, but this woman doesn't need to know we have lost control of the bat situation. We're the fire department, we're the ambulance team. We're the first responders, right? When we show up, people need to feel safe, and if Carol saw me laid up on my back on her over-stuffed floral couch with lace stuck to my cheek and my partner stuck to my front, I'm sure she'd have second thoughts about calling us for help tonight.

Sitting up, my forehead slams into Reid's.

"Ow! Seriously?" My hand flies to my forehead and I look at him only to catch Reid staring at my lips. Worried I've now managed to bust a lip, my hand finds its way south and taps around my mouth. "Am I bleeding or something?"

"Nope." Reid's cheeks flush red as he untangles himself

and jumps up, holding out his hand and pulling me up with him. "Thought you were, but you're not." Suddenly distracted, his eyes flick toward the front door. "Well, would you look at that?"

I glance over in just enough time to witness one stray bat winging his way out the front door of Carol's home. The tension in my shoulders eases, allowing them to slide down my back and be normal again.

Exchanging a knowing grin with Reid, I lean down under the console table. "Carol, it's safe to come out now."

Since we left Carol's, Reid's been stuck in a loop, laughing about the call. "That was nothing short of amazing."

"Glad we were able to keep you entertained, sir." Closing my clipboard, I hand it over for him to deal with. "Report is drafted. Can you sign it for me and I'll drop it on Jack's desk when we get back to the station?"

"Yep." Reid takes the clipboard from my hands and opens it, thumbing through the report I'd written up for our callout. He scans it, his eyes still lit up, and chuckles. "I mean, who would've thought there was a bat there?"

"Not me, but glad we could help." Placing the key in the starter, I rev the engine, touching the small lump beginning to form on my forehead. "I've always said you had a hard head, but dude. You have a *hard* head! I've got a giant knot forming now to prove it."

"Please. I'm going to have a lump, too. And you may have pulled a ligament in my pointer finger." Reid holds up his right hand and flexes his index finger, as if proving his point. "It's not the same as BB."

"BB?" He's got me. I'm curious now. "What is BB?"

"Oh, you know." Reid fiddles with the radio, settling on a local station with the volume set low. "Before Bat."

While Reid laughs at his amazing Dad joke—he's, like, the king of them—I put the ambulance in drive and begin a much saner course back to the station, as opposed to the hectic way we arrived. Pulling away from the curb, I point to my planner, which sits snug in its spot on the dashboard.

"Can you do me a favor and open my planner up and check today's date for me? I want to make sure I don't have anything else I need to do for work, so I can go home as soon as we're back."

Grabbing the planner, Reid grins as he opens it. "You love this thing, don't you?"

"Love it? I would marry it if I could." I'm joking, but I *am* an organized person, and Reid knows this. And while I'm organized, I've never gotten into using tech for organization, like to-do apps or the calendar on my phone. It has to be written. Reid did good when he gave me the planner as a surprise on January first this year. "That planner is my heart and soul."

Reid flips a few pages, landing on today's date. "Your to-do list looks clear to me, but tomorrow is another thing." He holds up the planner in my direction, pointing to the words written in all caps that say WING NIGHT. "I love a woman who is serious about wing night."

"I am always going to be serious about Wednesday wing night. Especially those honey wings! The best I've ever tasted. Thank you to Culture Shock for telling us about it, right?"

I hold up a hand for Reid to high-five, which he does complete with an eye roll. "Yes, thank you Culture Shock."

He teases, but even Reid knows that if it wasn't for Culture Shock, we'd not have any kind of a social life in this region. Culture Shock is a column about local art and culture news––it keeps a finger on the pulse of the greater community and treats readers to write-ups and reviews of hot spots to check out in the area. It isn't just any weekly column, it's *the* weekly column, and it's written for our local paper, the *Lake Lorelei News Post*, by someone named Andrew Jenkins.

I say someone because no one really knows who he is, but he seems to be everywhere. For the past year, he's been reviewing and rating all kinds of epic things to do in the area, from Lake Lorelei to Sweetkiss Creek and beyond.

And he's my favorite news source—not that it's news he's giving us, but you get my drift. If I need to read the paper, I do it on the day his column is published. "Gotta love the barbeque wings, dash of hot sauce, please."

Reid chuckles. "One day, you'll graduate to extra hectic heat, and when you do, I'll be there with the milk to temper your tastebuds."

In a flash, I'm pulling the ambulance back into its bay at the station and we're ready to call it a night. We both get out of the ambulance and make our way to our lockers, ready to do our end-of-shift paperwork before we go when our Lieutenant and acting chief for the next six weeks, Brett, approaches us.

"Hey, Shannon. Williams." He's the one man in here I let use my last name as my given name. With my dad also being a member of the same fire department, it can get confusing if we're both called Williams, but Brett manages to make it work. "Good night?"

"Interesting one," I manage, trying not to laugh. "And one we'll have to tell you about later, but I need to unwind a minute first."

"I need a good laugh, so please make sure you find me." Brett cracks a smile before turning to Reid. "Shannon, can I get a few minutes with you?"

Looking at Reid, I hold up the paperwork in my hands. "I can drop this off in the office, and if we need to deal with anything else, we can sort it out on the next shift."

"Thanks." Reid nods his head and grins at me. "Talk tomorrow?"

Nodding, I watch as they walk away from me, heading to the back of the station, probably to the kitchen, knowing them. Well, knowing Reid. After every callout, he needs to eat something.

The man is the best guy friend a girl could ever ask for. He eats his feelings; it's a coping mechanism. I've seen it happen over a department softball game loss as well as when he watched the last episode of *Game of Thrones*. It's why I can grin to myself now, knowing that when he gets into the kitchen, he'll find a batch of freshly steamed edamame from earlier today that I left in the fridge for him with his name on it—next to some Vietnamese vegetable spring rolls wrapped in rice paper. If he's going to emotionally eat, he needs to at least eat healthier.

Pulling my car keys out of my bag, my mind slips back to the memory of Reid staring at my lips earlier. It makes me stop in my tracks, a cold feeling rushing through me. It's like a cold flume of water, like a theme park ride with swishing and swirling, only this feeling also packs a little heat. Shaking my head, I push the thoughts that threaten to creep to the surface back again, because I'm still not ready to deal with them. Nope.

So Reid's been the best friend a girl could have after moving to a new town, so what? I can't even process the thought because I'm hit with the scent of fresh sheets and sandalwood. Only takes a moment for me to realize it's Reid. Must be his aftershave on my skin after that callout, and no, I don't mind it. Not one bit.

Am I struggling with the fact I've got some serious big-time feelings for my best friend? Yes, and I have been for a while now.

It started at a wedding, like all good stories do, a few

months ago. I'd felt a pull—more like an attraction—to this man, which hit me out of nowhere. He's someone I've known forever, well, if forever is two years, but it's been a busy two years since I moved here.

I'd chalked the feelings I had up to the fact we'd been at a wedding. You can't be surrounded by that much love and not get things a little twisted sometimes, right?

But the next day, after the wedding, I'd woken up and realized I couldn't stop thinking about Reid and how as he held me close when we danced, his thumb caressed my lower back and his breath hit my cheek....

It was then I realized this was bad.

And now I *know* I'm falling in love with my best friend.

TWO

Reid

When your boss asks you to do something, you're supposed to do it, right? I mean, a favor is one thing. Can I get a ride to the airport, may I borrow your car...? Heck, if he needed twenty bucks, I'm game.

But hang out with his sister who just moved to town?

"Let me get this straight." Crossing my arms, I lean back in my chair, weighing up my options. "Jack leaves for a six-week training course in Washington state, and his last act before leaving you in charge is to get you to ask me to hang with Etta? Like, you want me to hang with my boss's sister?"

Eyebrows arched, Brett inclines his head in my direction. "When you put it like that, Shannon, it sounds really weird and overly complicated. I think our good chief just wants you to keep her company, introduce her to some people who aren't her family. Like that Culture Shock column...show her the cool places to go."

A weird pit forms in my stomach, and I'm not sure why, but I do know it started as soon as Brett brought this whole topic up.

"I mean, I can. It's no problem, really. Just not sure why me?"

Brett shrugs one shoulder as he walks back across the floor to his desk and starts sorting a stack of papers. "He said you two met at his wedding and she's brought you up a few times, asking questions about you." Brett winks. "You must have made one stellar impression, Shannon."

"Questions about me?" It's true, I'd met Etta, Jack's twin, briefly at his wedding. We'd danced and had a few laughs that night, but I'll be honest—there was only one person at that wedding I was interested in. Spoiler alert: it's not my boss's sister.

Brett flips a hand in the air, like waving away the absurdity of my asking. "Yes, questions. But don't ask me what kind; I'm the messenger for the Chief and that's all."

"And you don't know why I'm the one he wants to do it?"

Brett pulls his glasses off, sits back in his chair, and runs his fingers through his hair. "I have no idea. I have a list here of things I need to do, and one of them was to relay this info to you from Jack." Sighing, he puts his glasses back on and looks me dead in the eye. "You just need to say hello, maybe escort her to something. I don't know. Be a good neighbor or something, would ya?"

"But, I'm confused." This happens often, more often than I care to admit. But it's one of the reasons Dylan says I have charisma, so I have that going for me. "Is it an order? Or am I to answer some questions about the best places to go eat on holiday weekends?"

"The girl is trying to get to know people. I'm sure she's going to have questions. She's been around here asking about all of us. She also asked if there was a good place to get a bikini wax in Lake Lorelei. However, I can't answer that question because I don't get those. Maybe you know someone you can introduce her to who can help her."

Brett stops sorting his paperwork and folds his arms in front of his chest. "Look, Shannon, I'm trying to help my boss get his twin sister settled in. She's a little nervous and has asked questions about you, Dylan, that guy who works as a volunteer three days a week named Hal…"

"Hal." I chuckle. That guy. Always the one you want on your trivia team, he knows the most useless information ever. "He's awesome."

"He is, but he also likes to darn his own socks in his spare time, as well as his mother's. I'm not feeling like he's a good fit as a first friend in a new town, you know?"

That pit in my stomach ebbs and flows. Someone must have added coffee to it. Feels like a spin cycle has been turned on and is coursing around my insides. I have no clue why I'm having such a strong reaction to this, but my body is physically rejecting this request.

I like Etta. She's nice enough. She talked my ear off about wine and what pairs best with a 2008 cabernet from Sonoma. She's also a fan of baseball, which was cool to find out. The only other woman I've ever known to be into baseball like I am is Dylan.

Dylan. If I'm thinking about baseball and Dylan, then she is my Field of Dreams. She's going to give me so much grief when I tell her about this at wing night. She'll probably laugh so hard that I have to play babysitter to the boss's sister that she'll choke on a chicken wing. Which would actually be horrible, but I know how to do the Heimlich. I'm an ambulance driver after all. But this thought leads me to thinking about her lips, which takes me veering off course.

"Yo, Shannon." Brett snaps his fingers in front of my nose. "Where'd you go?"

"Sorry." I shake my head from side to side, realizing my inner monologue forced me to check out for a second there. "Just got a lot on my mind."

"I get it." Brett eyes me with some suspicion, but then forges ahead. "So, can I give Etta your number and tell her to give you a call this week?"

"She's here?"

"Arrived last night. She's getting settled in, looking for a house and trying to figure out her next move."

We're both startled when the phone on Brett's desk rings loudly. I'm grateful for an out. "You need to answer that?"

Brett peers at the number on the screen and nods, looking back at me as he reaches across the desk to pick it up. "Yeah, I need to take this. So, can I pass on your number?"

Something about the time pressure of the phone ringing and my need to get out of the office forces my head to nod.

Slowly I back out of the office, being careful to shut the door behind me quietly. I stupidly think that by leaving the office, the washing machine in my belly would chill out, but it seems it's only sped things up.

I shouldn't feel this weird about hanging out with Jack's sister, but I do. Turning on my heel, I head back downstairs to the lockers so I can grab my duffle bag and head home, but I can't shake something.

And I think it's the reason I'm having a hard time with this request.

Dylan.

"Will you have the next column ready to go if I stop by tomorrow and grab it from you?"

My sister's voice is strained, even over the phone. Ari gets like this when she's under a time crunch with deadlines. Now that she's the editor of the *Lake Lorelei News*, her voice sounds like this pretty often these days.

"Yes, ma'am. The new column for Culture Shock will be

ready for your editing magic." I close the door to my refrigerator and lean against it. "In fact, I have two of them ready for you, that's how far ahead I am now."

"Ohhh, two articles for the paper at once! I'm so impressed." Ari manages a giggle. "Seriously though, can you believe how popular our little experiment is? I love this for you!"

"It is crazy, isn't it?" A few months back, I had dutifully listened to my sister's plans for the newspaper she runs. She'd spent a whole afternoon talking my ear off about her plans for it.

One of the new additions she implemented was adding a slew of local columnists to the roster, to help report local events and news but giving a less formal approach. Something written in layman's terms, she wanted these articles to be full of humor and insight, like a friend who had called and was telling you about something they had done or a story they'd heard.

"So, these columns will be like getting inside tidbits or the gossip from one of your friends, you know?" she'd said to me over my famous—to me and the crew at the fire station—chili. "Like, it'd be cool to get one of the parents to report on events for the schools, someone who is really into sports to write up local sports news, or a local chef to give cooking tips. That kind of thing."

"There's also rating and reviewing local businesses, too." I'd been listening to her wax on about this and had come up with my own idea to throw on the pile. "Maybe I could put my associate's degree to use and could do something to help, you know?"

Ari's eyes had narrowed, and she'd eyed me with suspicion. "Like what?"

"Well, I like going out and checking out new businesses when they open up. I could write about them. Give my perspective of what they are, what they do. Try out the new business and rate it...that kind of thing."

Ari had laughed, but she turned serious pretty fast. "Actually, it's not that weird of a pitch."

Imagine my surprise. "What?"

"You. Writing a column for the paper. You could write up reviews of events happening in the area at art galleries or museums, restaurant openings, any new adventure business that opens—that kind of thing."

"Really?" So my idea wasn't half-baked? "Do you think people want to know what I think about these things?"

"You and Dylan are always going out to stuff like this. Remember when that place opened where you bring a bottle of wine and paint a picture, and you two went because you insisted you had to check it out? I still have your painting hanging in our living room over the mantle of the fireplace, thank you very much."

"True, but to be fair, Dylan talked me into going."

"Semantics." Ari crossed her arms in front of her chest. "There's also the other time you two went to Suds and Buds, the new microbrewery where you can also do your laundry. Hearing you talk about that place made me go the very next day! Come on, Reid. Let's try it, just for a little bit. Please? For me?"

And so it was. That's the night Andrew Jenkins was born. But there's a catch, you see; when I agreed to do this, I laid down some rules. Well, one very solid rule.

He's a secret.

No one, and I mean NO ONE, but my sister knows that I'm the man behind Culture Shock. Not even Dylan, and I tell her everything.

Ari breathes out heavily in my ear, bringing me back to the present moment. "I love that we get to work together, but man, I can't wait until you finally start telling people that you are Andrew Jenkins. The guys at the firehouse are certainly going to freak, and our parents might pass out. Do you know they've been raving about the corn maze you wrote about in the fall?"

"No way." My cheeks go hot; it's an awesome moment for me when I hear I've made my parents proud. Especially when I feel like I've failed them as I've ventured out into adulting so far.

"They ended up going to that maze based on your column, you know. They almost missed a meeting at church because of it."

"Would not look good for the minister of the local church to be late for his own meeting, now would it?" Was I grinning? You bet I was. Knowing that something I did was bringing so many people joy, and one person in particular, was another reason I wanted to keep this identity a secret.

"Are you ever going to tell them—or Dylan for that matter?"

As soon as Ari says her name, an image of the most beautiful pillow-like lips springs to my mind. Again. An image that sends heat through my body but also takes the wind right out of me at the same time.

Dylan had stumbled into me on our call at Carol's house, and somehow those lips became the highlight of that moment. Like someone turned on a spotlight and shined it on the most perfect pink mouth, shaped like Cupid's bow, just for me to see and enjoy.

My stomach. The washing machine. It's back and it's flipping and swishing like a river after a rainstorm. I need to get these thoughts about Dylan out of my head, though, just for now. She's my friend. My best friend.

"I...well. I plan on telling Dylan and our parents." There, that should stop Ari for now.

"Good. When?"

Dang it. She is so pushy. "Soon?"

"How soon?"

Sighing, I tap my tongue on the roof of my mouth. "Like, in the next few...years?"

"Reid." Ari is quiet for a second before she does this thing —and she well knows it annoys me—where she *tsks* me. "Tsk, tsk, tsk."

"Don't you tsk me."

"Oh...*TSK*. You need to tell Mom and Dad at least. Especially Dad."

Telling my dad, well. I would like to tell him, I really would, but... Father has been giving me grief about not putting my degree to good use—his words not mine—and asking me if I might want to do more with my life.

Of course he has, he's my dad. I got my associate's at the community college, intending to take a few years off until I figured out what I wanted to do, but I also found the fire department at that time.

Does he support me and my decision to stay in the fire department? Yes, he's community minded and knows I love doing it. But does he want me to go back to school, get a bachelor's degree, do something more with myself? Going by the subtle hints he's dropped recently, it appears that he does. Hints like sending me pamphlets a few months ago for a four-year college that I could go to in-state.

I get it, he wants the best for me, but I need to figure out exactly what that is and what it means to me, and right now, it's writing. Something I never thought I'd be into or even good at, thus the reason I want to stay anonymous. It's a lot easier to hide behind Andrew than it is to show up as Reid. Plus, this writing gig? Turns out I'm digging it.

"I'll tell Dad soon, don't worry." Opening the top drawer next to the oven, I pull out a small folder filled with takeout menus. All sorted alphabetically by ethnicity, courtesy of

Dylan. "But for right now, I'm going to order a Thai red curry and some spring rolls, then get to bed early."

"Hm. Wing of Glory night tomorrow, huh?"

Tossing the menu on the counter, I can't help but roll my eyes. "Yes, it is. Why? You want to join us?"

"A double date with you and your unrequited love?"

"She's my friend, Ari."

"A friend you do everything with? I have one of those. I call him my husband."

I press my mouth close to the phone and make crackling sounds. "Cracswichblurg...Ari? Can you hear... cucshkkkklinggg...are you there? Ari?..."

"We both know you're not out of cell range." Her laugh floats through the phone and into the air surrounding me. "Fine, fine. I'll stop. But I'll see you tomorrow. I'll swing by the station and grab your articles from you."

"There's this thing called email..."

"Is it a crime to want to see my brother?" she growls.

Time to say goodbye. "See you tomorrow."

Once we disconnect, I fight the urge to not pat myself on the back. I'm guilty, sometimes, of doing things in a brotherly fashion in order to irritate my sister. It makes her crazy, but to me it keeps our sibling relationship intact.

Swiping through my contacts, I find the phone number and call my order in. Well, it's not *my* order but the order I usually do with Dylan. Only when we eat together, we get the mushrooms on the side.

Order placed, I flip the switch for the overhead light in the hallway and make my way to the bedroom. The hall used to be painted a dark navy blue, which I kinda liked at first, but after living here a few months realized it felt super dark and made the hallway feel smaller than it already was. Leave it to Dylan: she'd shown up one day with a couple gallons of white paint, some paintbrushes, and a playlist. It took four coats of paint and the whole weekend, but we'd gotten it done. And I would not have even started it if it wasn't for her urging and basically showing up with everything I needed. Like the paint-fairy of my dreams.

The woman knows how to show up for those she holds most dear. I've witnessed her being there for her father, for our friends at work, but most of all, she's always been right here beside me. We're partners at work, and when we're not on the clock, I feel lost when she's not around.

The only part where I'm confused is the part where I actually talk to Dylan about how I feel. I want to tell her when she's not near me, she's in my thoughts. I look around at the space I'm in, and she's saturated it with her Dylan-ness.

When I'm in my bedroom, I see the desk we put together from Ikea and smile remembering how she rocked that flat pack like nobody's business. When I'm in my backyard, I see the flower bed she planted for me and it makes my heart skip actual beats. I want to tell her that when I walk around my home, inside and out, I see her everywhere.

I just want her to see that there may be a future—and a really good one at that—with me.

THREE

Dylan

Crossing the threshold of the Sweetkiss Coffee Shop, a wall of noise rises to greet me. Familiar faces at most every table smile or wave as I thread my way across the room to the counter.

My father moved to the area—to the next town over called Lake Lorelei—a few years back. At his request, when he needed help, I followed him from Los Angeles so I could pitch in with the business he runs part time, a local car garage. While it meant he was able to keep a part time job for the Lake Lorelei fire department because I did, it also meant I was leaving my safety network and the job I loved, but it's all worked out so far.

I love this area, but mostly I love the little town of Sweetkiss Creek. So much that I've spent a lot of time here lately looking at places to live for when I do move out of my dad's, and hanging out with friends like the one I'm here to see today.

"There you are!" Riley sings out as she waves a hand in the air around her. "It's been manic here today. I haven't even had time for a break."

"Then take one with me now." Sliding onto one of the stools at the counter, I pat the empty seat beside me. "I can't eat my pie alone."

Riley Richards is the closest I can get to a sister from another mister in this town. As an outsider moving to a tight knit community like this one, I knew it was going to be hard to meet new people. Everyone wonders about the city girl showing up, thinking she's better than anyone else—and for the record, this is not me.

Riley and I had met at the local record shop when she worked there. I'd gone in looking for new vinyl to add to my collection and she recommended some old albums from Fleetwood Mac, Foreigner, and a greatest hits album from the Rolling Stones I hadn't seen before. We'd bonded over Stevie Nicks' voice, discussed the discography and true existential meaning behind most of R.E.M.'s albums, and found a shared love of Harry Styles. I know that last one is out of the blue, but come on. "As It Was" is a great tune.

Riley casts emerald eyes around the restaurant, smoothing back raven hair as she takes in the customers who are still in their seats. Watching her colleagues deftly take care of everything, I see her shoulders visibly relax and her expression follows suit.

"Fine." Riley disappears, crouching down behind the counter for a quick second before popping back up with a pie plate in one hand and a wine bottle in the other. Since her parents own the coffee shop, she's allowed some perks. "It's a nice day. Want to sit out on the patio?"

In a matter of minutes, we're outside sitting side by side, eating straight off the pie plate. Heaven.

"So," she manages between bites. "Are we making plans this weekend?"

"You bet we are. I need to celebrate." Pulling out my cell phone, I bring up my favorite spot online to get ideas for weekend plans. "It's not often someone pays off their last student loan now, is it?"

"Wheeee!" Riley squeals, throwing her hands in the air. "It's official! You're kind of debt free now, right?"

"I wouldn't call it debt free, but the albatross called 'student loan' is gone." I clink my wine glass with hers. "And I have some money saved for a down payment on a house. I still have miles to go, but every little bit helps. I've been watching the Sweetkiss housing market to get an idea of what to expect."

"You're so smart. I'm really excited—you can start looking for places here soon!" She stabs her pie with her fork, holding it aloft. "I bet your dad is so stinking proud of you."

"One hundred percent." He's been distracted lately, and I'm not sure what that's about, but he did take time the other night to mark the occasion with me over dinner. "I think he's in shock that I did it. I mean, I am too."

"Scrimping and saving is not for the faint of heart." Riley swallows her bite and points to the phone still in my hand. "So, how are we celebrating?"

"My faux boyfriend says there's an art gallery opening down the street tomorrow night. Want to go?"

"You live and die by that art and culture blog, don't you?"

"Mmmm. I think it's called a column."

"Well, I think you have a weird crush on some guy you've never met." Riley licks her fork and holds it aloft, using it as a conductor of a symphony would use his baton. "Correction. Some *blogger* you've never met."

The never-ending jokes from this one. "Andrew happens to be a source of happiness for me. My friends, like you, also reap the rewards of his wise words. How else would we have known to go to the Fajita Margarita night at Wholly Frijoles last week? Margs for four dollars and a fajita plate for ten. Tell me where else we would have gone?"

"You've got a point," Riley admits, albeit with a touch of sarcasm. "Still. You've got the hots for a guy you've never met."

"Who's got a crush on some guy she doesn't know?" someone says from behind me. Turning around, I find Etta standing there, holding a to-go coffee in her hands. "Is there a love connection I need to know about?"

"Twice in one week, I think you're officially a regular now." Riley tilts her head my way at the same time my foot is trying to kick her under the table. "Etta, this is Dylan, my friend who adores the way some local dude writes his blog."

"Column," I announce with a sigh. "Get it right."

"Whatever. " Riley kicks a chair out for Etta. "Want to sit down with us?"

"Sure," Etta says with a grin before turning to me. "We met at my brother's wedding, didn't we?"

"Guilty." I hold up my glass of wine, toasting no one. We did meet, and then she asked me if Reid was single, so forgive me if I'm not rolling out the red carpet at this very moment.

"And you've got a crush on someone you haven't met?"

I shoot Riley my sternest look only to be met with laughter. "It's not a crush. Andrew writes for the local paper. Thanks to him, we have a social life."

"And he likes to send Dylan subliminal messages through his writing. Or at least she thinks he does."

"Oh stop it, I don't think that." I smack Riley's arms with a gentle tap. "Fall in line, please."

Beside me Riley squirms as she giggles. "We're going to an art gallery opening tomorrow because Andrew said so. You should join us, Etta."

"You know, I'd love to." She smiles a perfect toothy grin, like she'd just won the Miss America pageant. Her brother has one of the most amazing smiles I've ever seen, so of course his twin sister would be just as striking. "That's so exciting! My first girls' night out."

"You know, if it's the Gallery on the Creek we're going to, I've met the new owners, the Stolls. Amelia, the wife, is incredible. She used to be an executive working in film and he's Spencer Stoll."

"The actor?" Etta whispers like it's supposed to be a secret.

Riley nods as she stands up and starts wiping down the tables around us. "Word on the street is they're planning to come into the area and invest some serious money into local businesses."

I'd read the same article in the paper recently about the new owners of the art gallery. The article was all about their life before moving here—after Spencer had decided to step away from the limelight and the glare of Hollywood, they lived in New England for a while and owned a construction business. They bought a nice lot on the edge of the lake and are currently building their dream home. I think I want to be like them when I grow up.

"Sweetkiss Creek could use an injection of funds like they have, but we'll see." It's not that I doubt them, it's that everyone wants to come here and invest once they stumble on the area. I've seen it happen in Lake Lorelei, so of course it's going to trickle over into neighboring townships like Sweetkiss Creek. The whole region is a real-life slice of heaven, and intruders want to bottle it for themselves.

Etta nods, eyeing me. "I've been looking at houses over here, but wow. This town could use some reinvention."

"More like intervention." Riley laughs. "But that laundromat mixed with a microbrewery brings in tourists and college students from surrounding towns, plus there's an amazing ice cream shop right by it."

"Well, you can count me in for a night out with you

ladies." Etta turns to Riley and points at her watch. "What time do you have?"

"Half past two."

"I need to go. I'm meeting one of my brother's friends today." She looks at me, rocking her head to one side. "Your friend. Reid."

"Reid?" Riley shoots me a covert sideways look before she goes back to wiping down the table in front of her like it's a ticking bomb and she needs to be the one to stop it.

"He's funny and seems like a good person." Etta shrugs a shoulder and looks at me. "I guess moving here, it's nice to meet someone and make a possible connection, you know?"

While I'm sitting here, hoping I look to the outside world like I'm amazingly calm, in reality part of me is out of my body and floating above us. Taking this in. Looking down at this scene as it plays out.

I change focus and swirl my glass of wine, staring into it like it's a crystal ball about to tell me my future, when Riley taps my shoulder. I look up to find her and Etta looking at me —Riley squints my way and Etta's brow is furrowed.

"You okay?" Riley asks as she walks past me and pats my shoulder.

"Yeah, sorry. I zoned out for a second." I smear a fake smile across my face and raise my wine glass. "Long day."

Etta smiles in my direction before she turns back to follow Riley, who is currently working her way around the patio, polishing one table at a time. "Should I get your number so I can call you about ladies' night?"

Pulling a pen out of her pocket, Riley finds a stray piece of paper and scribbles her number on it, handing it off to Etta. "Here. Text me when you can and we'll coordinate all the details, sound good?"

"Sounds great. See you guys," Etta says, throwing one last wave before she leaves.

I watch Etta until she disappears from sight, then turn back to Riley, who stands firmly planted in her spot, arms folded, and staring me down.

"Don't look at me like that." I wave off her glower. "Has she officially moved here now? I thought she was working for a winery and, like, happy where she was living."

Riley shrugs. "Etta said she sold half of her winery, so she's using the money to come down here and start over. She's talked about opening a wine shop here in town. Tasting room and events. That kind of thing."

"Well, that would be cool to have." I can't get mad at a tasting room. Even if it is *her* idea.

"Don't change the subject you know I'm about to bring up." Riley flicks me with her wet towel, snapping it lightly against my leg. "I know you have feelings for Reid. Are you going to let someone else sashay in here and take your man?"

"We have no idea if she wants to steal him, not that he's mine to be taken." I could hem and haw. I really could. I could give some excuse here as to why I'm not even trying to admit these feelings myself, but it's Riley. "So, since he's not my man, there's really no point, is there?"

"The point is that you tell Etta to lay off your man...I mean, if you want to." Riley shrugs as she bends down behind the counter and pops back up again. "I can only point out what I see, and I see two people who should be together."

A swirling feeling hits my stomach. Ever since Etta showed up and saw Reid, my tummy has felt like otters are having a splash party inside of it. I mean, what am I supposed to do here?

Reid Shannon is not the kind of guy I was expecting to ever be friends with, much less fall for. I loved my life in L.A., but when my dad decided to move to Lake Lorelei a few years ago, I ended up coming, too. My mother had walked out on us years ago when I was a little girl, so it's always been just us. Me and my dad, fighting the good fight together.

I met Reid the day I landed because Dad couldn't make it to the airport. He'd been called out for a fire emergency, so he'd sent Reid in his place. Reid had just joined the fire department and was taking classes to drive the ambulance. I'd just finished my paramedic training and was starting at the Lake Lorelei Fire Department soon. It was only a matter of weeks before we became partners, and the rest is...well, the rest is now.

"You don't see the point of what I'm saying, but I do." Standing up, I make my way over to the outdoor server station where Riley stands with a hand on her hip. "I left a tight group of support back in Cali when I came here. Making a friend like Reid was like getting a life preserver. We've worked hard on our friendship, plus we work together. I don't want to screw everything up because I have feelings."

"Oofff, you're a mess. I'd suggest you go to the local therapist, but sadly she moved to Florida about a month ago."

"There's not a therapist in the area? That would not go over well in L.A." Pointing to the clock on the wall, I grab my things. "Shoot. I need to get to the garage. Dad's getting some help from that accountant you recommended; in fact, they met today. Thanks again for that. He even texted and said he has news for me."

"I hope Benny can help. He helped me when I thought the IRS was coming down hard and I felt threatened. Hopefully he can help your dad, too."

I grab a nearby pitcher of water, pour myself a glass, and chug it. "I need to get going or I'll be late for wing night."

Riley shakes her head. "You had to mention wing night with Reid, didn't you?"

"I didn't even say Reid's name." Sighing I roll my eyes. "Am I being weird?"

"You're always weird."

"No, but like, weird. You know." I look at her and shake my hands in front of me. "Weird. About Reid."

Riley stops mid-wipe and turns to me. "You're always weird when it comes to him. And it's fine. People are weird when they're in love."

Rolling my eyes, I turn to go. "I'm leaving now."

"Fine. Go be weird––with Reid."

I don't know why, but at the mention of his name, I have a jerking reaction with my hand at the same time I think an eyelash gets stuck in my eye. My left hand flies to my face, trying to stop the pain in my eyeball, while my right hand manages to wipe the salt and pepper shakers, a bowl of sugars and alternative sweeteners, a cruet of soy sauce, and a bottle of ketchup off a table.

Everything crashes to the ground around me, but success. I think I got the eyelash out.

"Yeah, you're not being weird. Not at all." Riley stands by the mess with a hand on her hip. "Get outta here, will ya?"

"Sorry, Riley." I start to help, but she waves me away.

"You've done enough. Go. Wing night, all that jazz."

Waving goodbye, I make way back inside through the cafe and swing the main door open, stepping out onto the semi-bustling sidewalk of Sweetkiss Creek. Pulling my car keys from my pocket, I head down the street to my car. My dad's garage is in Lake Lorelei, and I've got about ten minutes until I'm there.

Plenty of time for me to be alone with my thoughts. Like the persistent one where Reid and Etta are dating and I become a lonely, sad third wheel.

Sticking the key in the ignition, I realize that alone time with my thoughts is overrated.

FOUR
Reid

Seeing my sister stand beside Truck 41 with her arms crossed tightly in front of her is not the blissful way I want to end my daily one-mile run. Judging by the smirk on her face and the Batman logo on her T-shirt, she's heard about my adventure yesterday with Dylan.

"Oh, lookie here." She gives me one of those all-knowing sisterly expressions that says I'm judging you but also not really. "It's the Batman."

"I guess if I need to be a superhero, I'll take Batman." I kick my leg up onto a rung near her head, impressing her with my agility, I'm sure. Knowing her penchant for a certain comic book character, I hit low. "Much better than that sissy from outer space, the one with the big S on his chest, right?"

"You need to leave Superman alone. We've had this conversation." Ari smacks my arm before tossing her hair out of her face and over her shoulder. "Be warned, Dad is in the vicinity."

"Oh?" This isn't a bad surprise, just not one I'm expecting today. "Any special occasion?"

"Not sure." She tilts her chin toward the closed door to

the Lieutenant's office, which is located on the other side of the truck bay. "He's with Brett now."

"He's probably requesting I get time off so he can try to guilt me into getting a bachelor's."

Ari rolls her eyes at me, again, in a way that only your sister can. "I doubt it's that reason. Honestly, it's a sad song you sing, you need to let it go. I don't think he cares as much as you do."

Opening my locker, I take out my car keys and cell phone, tossing the keys in the air. "I can't worry about that right now —I need to find a roommate first."

"You still haven't found anyone?"

"Not yet, but give me time. If I don't, I guess I'll have to move out."

Ari chuckles. "Or back in with Mom and Dad."

As the last word drops from her lips, a voice behind me speaks up. "Let's try not to have that happen."

Turning on my heel, I spin and find my dad, who is also our station chaplain, standing with Lieutenant Brett.

"Lieutenant. Hey, Dad." I tip my head in my father's direction. "Wasn't expecting to see you here today."

My father is a good-looking fella, and I'm not the kind of guy who notices these things about people. He's muscular for his age, the result of his weekly workout routine that he's stuck to for over thirty years. His mane of thick sandy-blond hair matches mine, and when I look into his eyes, it's like looking at a reflection. It's safe to say that based on genes, I know where my looks are headed over time. "It's not like I make my calendar known for all."

Laughing, Brett turns to acknowledge Ari before turning to my dad and shaking his hand. "Thanks again for stopping by, Pastor Shannon. Keep my friend in mind if you hear of any vacancies."

"Vacancy?" My ears perk up. "Like, a roommate kind of vacancy or job vacancy?"

"Could also be a storefront vacancy," Ari muses beside me. "Or a house."

Dad shoots his sternest look our way, used to our witty banter. Not that he thinks we're witty, but maybe one day. He turns to Brett, hands out, almost apologetic. "Sorry about these two. One is as bad as the other some days."

Smiling, Brett folds his arms in front of his chest and looks me up and down. "Why are you so curious about a vacancy of any discretion?"

"I've been trying to find a new roommate for a while now." Shoving my phone in my back pocket, I clasp my hands together behind me. "Not having much luck."

Brett and my dad exchange a knowing look. "Good timing. I've got a new volunteer from Beaufort coming up to work in the area. He's a police officer, and I think he's going to be stationed at Sweetkiss Creek." Opening his clipboard, he flips through some paper until he lands on the page he's after. "Isaac Wright."

"Zac?" Now it's my turn to try and stop the grin that won't stop. "I know Zac, we took a CPR course together last year and we've been on the same team for the Carolina Fire-fighter Competition before. He's awesome."

Brett's smile is huge as he pumps a fist in the air. "Even better. The police department will pay for his share of the rent for the first six months, if you're cool with him living with you until he can find a place in Sweetkiss Creek?"

"More than cool. I'm so cool, I'm like a watermelon that's been on ice in the back of the freezer for a year."

Dad looks at me like I have eight heads and my hair is on fire. "What?"

I shrug. "Cool as air conditioning?"

Judging by the way my audience is looking at me, my

attempt at a joke has fallen flat. I hold my hands up in surrender. "I was trying a thing, you guys."

Beside me Ari shakes her head. "Oh, man."

Dad's eyes bounce back and forth, watching Ari and me. I wonder if he's thinking how he got it so right with one of us, but the other one...well, I would assume he thinks the jury is still out.

He turns back to Brett, but not before casting one last stern look my way, and slaps his shoulder once. "Well, looks like my work here is done. Let me know if your new member needs anything from me, okay?"

Brett says goodbye and disappears around a fire truck off to be Lieutenant-y or something, and I sit down on a bench by the wall. When I look up, two sets of Shannon eyes are creepily watching me. It's off-putting.

"What?" As the word comes out, it slips out a bit sharper than I intend.

"Reid, not everything needs to be defended." My dad shifts from one foot to the other before he leans in and kisses Ari on the cheek. "I need to get going. I have a meeting at the church. Will I see you both soon for more than a few moments in passing?"

"You can count on it." She stands on her tiptoes and kisses him back.

He's making his way past me when he stops to give my shoulder a squeeze. "Maybe having a roommate means you can think about going back to school now. If you can't save the money, I'm sure you can apply for scholarships. I know plenty of other men your age who have gone back to school later and found it easier to both take the classes and to juggle their responsibilities."

It's time like this I wish he did know about me being Andrew. I want him to see I am doing something. I'm serving my community, like him, but also I'm writing. And I like it.

Could I rip off the Band-Aid and just tell him right now? Ari is here to back me up, and I can spill the beans. But I don't want to. Not yet. The timing has to be right.

So, I simply smile and respond, "We'll see."

Someone nearby clears their throat. "Am I interrupting a meeting or something?"

I don't even need to turn around to know it's Etta. She'd called me last night to say hi—probably given orders like I was —and mentioned she might stop by the station today. I glance to the side, and sure enough, there she is standing in the bay with her hand up in a half wave.

"Etta." My dad beams. "You're not interrupting anything. I'm on my way out. Nice to see you again."

"Same here." Etta steps forward and shakes his hand.

"I guess I'll talk to you soon." Dad stands awkwardly for a moment, watching each of us as we stand in an uncomfortable circle before he starts to back away. "Okay, then. Ari, call your mother."

I can't help the sigh of relief that escapes as soon as he's gone from our view. I love him, but I worry I'm not living up to what he wants me to be.

"If I knew you were both here, I would have grabbed you a couple of coffees from the Sweetkiss Cafe, too." Etta's teal blue eyes find mine and she smiles.

"I'm more of a chai latte kind of guy than coffee." I'd never heard of a chai anything until Dylan; now she's got me hooked on chai lattes. With almond milk, of all things. It's an order that I dig, but when I ask for the almond milk some-times, I admit, I whisper it. I'm still getting used to the idea of nuts as milk. "It's my favorite, actually."

"I'll need to remember that. For future." Etta punctuates her sentence with a wink before looking around. "I need to talk to Brett. Do you know where he is?"

"That way." Ari points in the direction where he headed. "He was walking to his office."

"Thanks, Ari. Nice to see you again." She turns to me, smiling. "So we'll make a plan soon to do something one day?"

"You betcha!" Am I a bit overly enthusiastic, almost shouting as she walks away? Totally.

Etta is no sooner gone from our little section of fire station real estate when a certain sister of mine spins on her heel to face me, raising an eyebrow in my direction.

"Did not have you pegged to go there..."

"Are you kidding?" I visibly shudder. "She's my boss's sister. No way."

Ari sighs. "Don't do it for that reason. Think of Carter and I..."

"Touché." An expression I can only describe as irritation crossed with exasperation makes its way across Ari's face. She's got a point. She did marry *my* best friend, Carter, but their marriage is the reason I've been looking for a roommate.

But she also knows Etta is the last woman I'm interested in.

"Look, jokes aside, she's really nice, but I don't have time right now to date anyone. I'm busy working on the ambulance, I have to keep up on my training if I want to move up in the department, and I'm also working for you. You are one tough boss to answer to."

"I get it, except for the part about me being tough. We need to talk about that." She wags a finger at me before continuing. "Seriously. If it's not going to be Etta, then I really wish you'd open your eyes and make a move. You already see what you have in front of you."

We're going here again. "If you're talking about Dylan—"

"Of course I'm talking about Dylan." Ari tosses her hands in the air. "What is up with men? Seriously, none of you know what you have until it's gone. She's a gem. You two get along so well, she laughs at your ridiculous jokes, and you actually listen to her."

"I'm not going to mess up my friendship with her because I have a crush—we work together." I couldn't be more serious about this very subject if I tried harder. "Plus, it's Dylan. I really don't think I'm her type."

"You never know unless you try." Ari leans in close to me, giving me this look she likes to give me when she thinks she's right. "I know a lot of things you would not be doing, at all, if you hadn't just tried. Speaking of which, do you have the write-up for me to put in the paper, Andrew?"

"In my locker." I incline my head toward the block of lockers along the brick wall behind her.

"Do you mind grabbing it for me?" Ari says slowly, her head nodding in agreement. "And since I'm your editor now for your top secret project, I figure I'll come by and pick up your articles each week. No need to email them. This way I get to see you."

I make my way over to my locker, opening it and reaching in for my backpack. "And if they aren't ready?"

Ari watches as I sift through the bag, pull out a folder, and hand it over into her waiting hands. "Then I'll have to beat you up in front of your workmates."

"Lame." I open my mouth to toss another barb her way, but instead the intercom system around me comes to life signaling a call.

"Call for an ambulance at 468 Oak Park Drive. Request for a fire engine to also arrive simultaneously for backup. That's 4-6-8 Oak Park Drive, man having chest pains."

The quiet area around us is now filled with alarms, fire-fighters, the on-duty paramedic team riding the ambulance today, and general chaos.

Stepping into my gear, I catch Ari's eye as she stands flat

against a wall. She's smart enough to stay out of the way and clear of us and the trucks so we can get out of here, and fast.

I'm not on duty, but I grab my gear and hop on a truck anyway. More hands are better than fewer...and it gets me out of talking about my love life and daily activities with my sister.

Pulling out of the station, I still hear her words echoing in my head about Dylan. But Ari doesn't know like I do that we're friends. And I don't want to mess up. My eyes fall on the small tattoo I have on the inside of my right wrist. It's small, a version of our department emblem surrounded by tiny flames. A present from Dylan when I mentioned to her how much I wanted a tattoo once.

Leaning my head against the seat of Truck 41, I close my eyes and see her. No matter where I am, it's her I want to be with.

But I need to be honest with myself and with my status in the friend zone. Firmly planted in Dylan's friend zone, for sure, but it's where I am.

It's just going to hurt if it ends up being where I stay.

FIVE

Dylan

The mechanic's garage is quiet when I arrive. Walking through the front door into the lobby, I make my way to the office where Kenny Loggins is singing about being footloose over the speakers. Good old *Footloose*, one of my dad's favorite movies of all time, and now that I've seen it with him probably thousands of times, I concur. Kevin Bacon is kinda amazing.

The tiny room is covered in a thin layer of dust, telling me it's been too long since I made time on my calendar to straighten it up. I make a mental note to give it some attention in the next few days.

Once I'm through the office and past the bathroom and supply closet, I step into the main garage where my dad, whose nickname is Dubs, stands with a forlorn look on his face. His real name is William, but somehow it got from William to Wills to Billy to W. to Dubbya to Dubs. He's always been known for having a smile that's sprinkled with a touch of grumpy, but he's pretty casual and laid-back for the most part. Seeing the expression that clouds his features now, I'm worried that his visit to the accountant Riley recommended didn't go well.

I call out first before scaring him to death, only someone else hears me first. There's a yelp of surprise when Max, my little terrier, runs inside from the back of the garage and jumps in my arms.

"You didn't have Max in here with you while you were working, did you, Pop?" I scoop my little man up, pulling him close to my chest. "You know we can't have him around the machinery."

"Like I can control that wild beast." His expression morphs, a huge smile filling the space where sadness was only a second ago.

Looking down at the tiny Muppet-like Care Bear I'm holding in my arms, I would hardly use terms like "wild" or "beast." This is my baby.

"Maxie is a good boy. You forget, he went to two puppy training classes."

"I love how you say that like it's an accomplishment," he grunts as he stands up straight and stretches his arm overhead. "You neglect the part where the second class was really the two of you having to take the first one over again because Max failed."

Swiftly, I cover Max's little ears. He's a Silky Terrier mixed with a little Cairn, so a very soft, golden-like version of Toto. Is he the most obedient? Nope. Not at all, but he's mine.

"I'm not here to be ridiculed, I'm here to do my job." Leaning over, I give him a peck on the cheek. "I'm heading into the office."

"Okay." He looks around the garage, making a motion with one of his hands, circling the air. "I'm going to straighten it up for the night, and then I'll come fill you in on the meeting today."

"Sounds good." I tip my head in the direction of the office.

"If you need me, I'll be right there in my cage. With the wild beast."

Marching back to the desk, I hold Max close and kiss his wee head, whispering in his ear that he's a good boy. I mean it when I say he's my baby. He was my first rescue when I lived on the west coast. I'd volunteered to help clean my local park one Saturday afternoon, and we'd found Maxie that day.

I'm still not sure if he was dumped there or a runaway, but we'd made signs and done all the things. We scanned him for a chip, which he didn't have, called local vets, and we even linked up with the SPCA and other rescues to see if anyone was looking for him. When no one stepped forward to claim him after two weeks, he became mine. I feel like my life got all the better from that moment on.

When I pull out the chair at the desk to sit down, some of my hair falls in my face, covering my eyes. Pushing the strands back, I get hit with a familiar scent of clean sheets and sandalwood. Tracing my day, I remember Reid spraying himself when I walked past him at the station earlier, which of course meant he had to spray me as well. Did I protest when he did it? Yes, but of course now that I'm sitting here getting little whiffs every time I move my head, I'm loving it.

Looking at the files on my desk that Dad has left for me to deal with, I settle in. I pull up Spotify and find a good playlist to have on in the background, because one needs ambiance when sending out invoices. Tapping on my keyboard, in a few strokes I've got the program I need pulled up, and I'm off. Time to catch up on the admin.

Time always flies when I sit down at this desk, like stepping into a time-space continuum where I think I've spent maybe ten minutes on something, but when I look at the clock, I'm always shocked to see it's more like an hour or two. This is the case today where what I think is a quick twenty-minute job turns into an hour task. It's Max's nose nudging my shin that pulls me away, drawing my eyes to the time.

"I know, Max, we need to go soon-ish." Reaching down, I scratch Max between the ears, then under his chin, which is his weak spot. He's back asleep in less than ten strokes, and I pull up my online news source, Culture Shock. Since Dad hasn't graced me with his presence yet, I figure I should indulge.

Clicking on Andrew's latest post, my happy place begins a low hum. I don't know Andrew Jenkins personally, but I dig his style. I like to think if Andrew and I ever met, we'd be good friends, maybe even the best...but I can't tell Reid that.

Sometimes Andrew gives his take on new bands that pop up at bars down the road. When Taylortown, which is about twenty minutes away, opened a food truck alley and started hosting open mic nights, Andrew went. He reviewed every food truck, all fifteen of them, and sent readers like myself on a mission where we needed to do the same, like a scavenger hunt for gluttons. Poor Reid, I made him go with me to each truck over the course of a few days' time, and I think we both gained five pounds.

I don't know, I can't explain it, but something about Andrew's adventures makes me feel like I need to do them, too. Like they're catered for me.

His latest comical write-up is about the new Sweetkiss Creek dog park that opened to the public last week, thanks to a petition put forth by yours truly and about one hundred other dog owners who longed for a safe space to let our pooches run free. Andrew had rallied behind us and helped spread the word in his columns. I'm pretty sure he used his platform to help us make this dog park happen. Maybe he's a dog lover, too? The thought makes me grin from ear to ear. So does the shout he gives me––well, that he gives to my alter ego puppylover915––in his column as well. How cool is that?

Immediately, I scroll to the comments, because of course I

have to leave one. I always do. Andrew shows up for me, so I will support. As puppylover915, I give him a thumbs-up and a thank you, promising to go to the dog park regularly to show my support for our little town. I'm sure Andrew could care less, but it's my way of saying thanks to him for bringing a little joy to my days.

Before I hit post, I make sure to add in an extra woo hoo for his write-up on the art gallery since I'm going to that as well because of him. As soon as I'm done, I re-read what I've written and, deeming it fit for posting, hit send before leaning back in the chair, feeling like I've had a day complete.

Movement at my feet brings my attention to Max under the desk. "Now we have to go try out the new dog park, Max. You in for an adventure with me?"

As if in agreement, Max side-eyes me before yawning, stretching, and rolling onto his back, showing me his pink tummy. *This. Dog.*

I hop up and start packing my things—except for Max, who will go home with Dad tonight since I have wing night—when my father knocks on the office door and pops his head through.

"Are you going now?"

I nod. "But I want to hear what happened today."

"Okay. Let me sit down." If I'm not mistaken, his voice sounds a little jittery, like he's nervous, which makes me twitchy immediately.

"Sure." I point to the small couch opposite the desk we share as I flop down onto it. "What's up?"

Dad plops down beside me. "So the meeting wasn't great."

"It wasn't?" I wondered if we should look around for more accountants. I pull my phone out and tap the Google app, typing in "accountants near me." "Let me see if we can find someone else, then..."

"The accountant Riley recommended was great, but it's

my situation that isn't." Leaning back heavily into the couch cushions, he sighs. "Basically, because of the issues with my back taxes, if I don't come up with the money in two months, I'll lose the garage."

"Oh." There's a not-so-nice feeling beginning to rise in the pit of my stomach. My poor father. He'd moved to the east coast before I finally made up my mind to come, too. It was actually at his asking that I moved. He'd opened the garage and didn't want to run it alone. And it had always been us since Mom left, so what's a girl gonna do? She's going to go and support her dad.

About the time I was thinking of moving here two years ago, he found out an accountant he had used years ago when he lived in California had not reported his income properly for over ten years. The accountant had long ago disappeared, and now my dad is left holding the bag and owing more money than either one of us can wrap our heads around.

"That's not the news I was expecting."

He dips his head lower. "Me, neither. It's bad, Dylan, and I don't have much time to try to fix it. I can make payments, but they still want a huge chunk of money now."

"Can you go to the bank and ask for a loan?"

He shrugs a shoulder. "I might, but I don't think they will. My credit score has taken a beating, too. My first step is to put the house on the market, but I wanted to run it past you before I did anything." Dark eyes watch me. "I know it may feel like this is coming from out of nowhere, but it's something I've been thinking about doing for a while."

"You have to sell the house?" I can barely form the words with my mouth. It's like my jaw unhinged and it's swaying below my face, my chin skimming my chest. "Where would you move?"

"Upstairs."

"Oh." Of course. I had forgotten about the two-bedroom

apartment above the garage. Probably because he's rented it out for the last few years. "But, I thought the tenant had signed a new lease recently?"

"He did, but he was offered a new job in Virginia, so he's moving in a few weeks." He manages a sad smile. "The timing seems right, so I thought we could move in there for now. It's small, but we can make it work with both of us in it."

Something in this doesn't feel right. My poor dad has to sell his house and he's worried about how I feel about sharing a two-bedroom with him?

"You don't have to worry about me." I stand up, pacing the floor, aware of Max keenly watching me. "If you need to sell the house, let's do it. I've been thinking of applying for full-time work, so I'll start sooner rather than later. I can pitch in extra money, plus I don't have my student loan debt hanging over my head." Realizing I have a stash I'd been saving for my first house, I snap my fingers. "I've got my house money, too. I can give you that to use."

"No, no." Dad holds up his hands, his cheeks flushed pink. "I can't have you do that. Not any of that, not at all. I'm your father, I should be the one taking care of you."

"You're my father, who brought me into and up in this world." Folding my arms across my chest, my mind is going a mile a minute. "I can start by finding a new place to stay. It's about time I flew out of the nest."

"Who says?"

"I do." At some point, I slow my racing mind down to a stop. "The more I think about it, the more sense it makes. You have the opportunity to downsize while trying to save your business."

"That's what I thought, too. No time like the present, I guess?"

Taking his hand, I pull him to stand and wrap my arms

around my dad, squeezing him close. "There is no time like now, and I'm here to help you in any way I can. Okay?"

He doesn't have to answer; the bright crimson color snaking its way across his neck and heading north says it all.

"Okay." Knowing what we have to do, I go back to packing my bag and getting Max ready to leave. "I'll make some calls to a few realtors and we can set some meetings up. I'm sure we can even get in front of someone tomorrow if you want to move that fast?"

"Well, actually..." I watch my dad's face go bright red once again. "There's more news, but this is good so I saved it for last."

"Oooookay." Slowly, I cross my arms in front of me. "What is it?"

He puts both hands on his hips and stands tall. "I've met someone."

"Did you say you met someone?" I don't think I heard him right. "Like someone in passing, a new doctor, or are we talking about a love interest?"

Narrowing his eyes, he shakes a finger in my direction. "She's local and we're not ready to tell anyone yet, so do me a favor and respect that for right now, okay?"

"Sheesh!" I hold up my hands in front of me like he's wielding a pistol in my direction and trying to rob me. "I'm fine with you dating, it's your life. In fact, I'm thrilled to hear that you are."

My voice trails off as a second wave of realization hits me. Everything is changing. Everything.

"The timing is horrible, but I'm seeing her as my shining light in the storm." Dad sticks his hands in his pockets, giving me an "oh shucks" vibe like I've not seen before. "She's pretty awesome, Dylan. Can't lie. She knows what I'm dealing with —the house, the garage, the taxes—and has already offered to help. I won't let her, but the fact she did offer was too kind."

"She sounds great. It must be serious for you to be telling me about it and if you've told her about what's going on with your finances." Part of me already knows the answer. This man has not ever dated anyone—not one single soul—since my mother left us. It's been years, and nada.

He reaches over and takes one of my hands and wraps it in both of his. "You will always be my number one, got that? There is not a woman on this earth that will ever come between me and my baby girl. In fact, if things keep going the way they are, this one is going to make our lives richer."

My heart does a flip, and I throw my arms around his neck. "Can't argue with that. You tell me when it's time to meet her, and I will."

"Thank you." He squeezes me tight, then pulls away. "You need to get going, don't you? I'm not gonna hold you up from your standing dinner date with Reid."

"I'm sure he'll appreciate it. The only way he can get the two-for-one special is if I'm there to share it with him." I wiggle my eyebrows at him. "Big night out."

"Enjoy it." He starts to walk out of the tiny office, but turns around like he forgot something. I'm surprised when he marches back up to me and wraps his arms around me again, pulling me in for a bear hug.

"I love you, Dyls. I'm sorry you have to deal with all of my bad choices right now when your mind should be unencumbered with this level of adulting."

"I mean it when I say I want to help you in any way I can." I sneak in an extra squeeze before he pulls away. "I'm telling ya, we've got this, Dad."

Watching him walk away, I feel that dip come back to my stomach. How can I tell him we've got this when I have no clue what it is we can do next?

There is no silver lining, at least not one I can see. If the bank won't help him, which they probably won't based on his credit history and the threat of the lien, I need to step up and help.

Everything is changing, and yet there's nothing I can do but hold on. That and pray for gravity to keep me in one spot, unmoving, so I can help that man weather this storm.

SIX

Dylan

"Y ou're really moving out?" The twisted look of confusion washing across Reid's face matches my insides perfectly. I'm glad it's not just me feeling like this has come out of the blue.

"We have to, Reid." A shiver snakes its way down my spine, causing goosebumps to appear, prickling along my flesh.

"Are you cold?" In an instant, Reid wraps his fire department-issued jacket around my shoulders. "You're shivering."

Our server stops by and drops off more of the famous Wings of Glory blue cheese dressing and an extra plate of carrot sticks and celery. I can't get mad at a crudité any day of the week. I snap up a carrot stick and dunk it in the dressing.

"It's a lot to take in. I mean, we went from horrible news to good news and back to the crappy news in less than five minutes. I'm just in shock for him and really sad that he's dealing with this, especially at his age."

Reid shakes his head, staring at the table in front of him. "I wish I could help."

"Me, too. In fact, if you figure out how we can rob a bank so I can give my dad some money, let me know. I'm in."

I feel his eyes watching me. "Do you know where you want to live—I'm assuming you'll stay local?"

"I'll see what I can afford. I've been looking for another job, like another part-time one to supplement the fire department, but now I'm thinking maybe I should get a full-time job somewhere so I can make more money, you know? Then I can feel like I'm helping him somehow if I contribute to this bill."

"You aren't thinking of going back to California are you?"

Had I thought about it? Yes, but only for a fraction of a second. I know I could go back there and get an event planning job, like I had before. I know the money I'd make and what I'd be going back to. It's familiar to me, and we have family there...but it's not here. It's not what I consider to be home now. But in times of crisis, you do what you have to do.

"I honestly don't know." I throw my hands in the air. "I offered to give him my house savings, but he won't take it. I just have no clue what to do to make this better."

Taking a sip of his iced tea, Reid nods. "I feel you, but I know you'll figure it out. Maybe he'll get a loan from the bank, like you said."

"It's going to be hard, Reid." Sighing, I shove a carrot dramatically in the bleu cheese dressing again before I aggressively take a bite of it. "He's not got a good credit score and banks want perfection. Dad is not perfection, he's rough edges and gristly bits wrapped in sunshine."

"You forgot that he rides on a unicorn and farts sprinkles."

Laughing, I reach across the table and touch one of the honey barbeque wings on Reid's plate. "Did you really want to eat that?"

He rolls his eyes and hands me his plate. "You know I don't want it now that you've put your mitts on it."

"Yes, that I do." I grin while taking his plate and remove my well-earned wing before handing his plate back to him. I take a bite and chew thoughtfully for a few minutes, silently weighing my options. Going back to California is always an option, not that I want to, but at least it's there. Having so much of my dad's family in Southern California is a blessing and could come in handy, but the thing is, I'm happy here. Right here on this side of the country.

Being a part of the fire department gives me that feeling of being on a team, a part of something bigger than me. Not quite like I would feel when I worked organizing and throwing events. Technically, yes, I was part of a team, but this is different.

This team is more like family. A giant dysfunctional family that teaches me what love and trust and patience mean every day. And they're mine.

And of course, Reid's here. There's that.

Without looking, I feel Reid watching me, paying attention to my every move. Snapping my eyes to Reid's, I find him staring at my lips. This again? My hand flies to my lips where I find a slathering of wing sauce across them. I confirm this by looking at my fingers before swiping a napkin and wiping the mess off my face.

Reid's cheeks flush pink as he clears his throat and shifts in his seat. "Do you have any family around besides your dad?"

It's like with so many things between us—of course Reid can read my mind. "In California. But I think that's my worst case scenario, you know?" Sighing, I pour myself a pint of beer from the small pitcher sitting on the table. "I only just got the news. We need to pack and get out of his house, and I still need to find time to start looking for a place while looking for a job. However, for today, I give up. I can only say thank you to Andrew Jenkins for turning us on to wing night at this place. I look forward to these nights with you. The best."

"I'll toast to that." Reid's our designated driver, so he

clinks his iced tea glass against my mug. "While we're toasting, here's to my new roommate. Brett texted me earlier and said he'd be moving in on Friday."

"Two days from now? That's awesome!" Smacking my glass into his, I plaster a fake smile across my face, wanting so badly to be able to fake-it-till-I-make it, but the empty clang inside me says not quite yet. "Good for you. At least one of us has our housing crisis solved."

"We'll figure yours out, too, Dylan, I promise."

Reid's face is so hopeful. I just hope he's right.

The sun is already in the midst of her slow retreat when I maneuver my car into the parking lot of the new fenced-in Sweetkiss Creek dog park. Max is in full whine and prancing mode, ready to fly out the passenger side door, through the gate, and into the green space where several of his new doggie friends wait for him anxiously.

Sitting down on a bench at the edge of the park, I unclip Max's leash from his harness and watch him as he tears down the small hill toward a waiting pack of like-size small dogs. He arrives, barking his head off, and is rewarded when the group barks in return. Overjoyed, the small gang takes off across the park, free as the wind.

"Is that seat beside you free?"

Unaware anyone was near me, I jumped at the sound of another person's voice. Glancing up, I find a striking tanned blonde woman looking at me as she pushes her sunglasses on top of her head.

"Sure." I move my purse from the empty seat.

"Thanks." She sits, but is still only for a moment. She waits a few minutes before turning to face me. When I look in her direction, she smiles in that overeager way someone does when they're waiting for you to give them attention.

"I'm new here and thought I'd come check out the park." She points to a beagle who was trying to sniff Max. "That's Barney. He's such a gentle guy. I'm glad they have a dog park here. He got used to them when we lived in L.A."

"I love those dog parks in Los Angeles. Max spent a lot of time at one in particular, in fact, he was what you would consider a regular in the doggy world. It was off a road called Laurel Canyon when I lived there." I point out Max, who now trails Barney across the grass. "That's Max."

"Well, I'm Amelia." She holds out her hand. "I think I saw you at the coffee shop here the other day?"

"Probably. It's not like we live in a metropolis, so you could have seen me anywhere. I think I heard through the small-town rumor mill that you and your husband moved here recently, right?"

"We did. We're settling into our home, here in Sweetkiss Creek, where we bought the art gallery. I'm also hoping we seal the deal on a new business this week." She pulls her sunglasses off her head and holds them in her hand. "I think I'm becoming a serial entrepreneur."

I grin. Amelia is easy to talk to. "There are worse things. Can I ask which business?"

"The Sweetkiss Campground. Do you know what a treasure that place is?"

You bet I do—it's the former jewel in the Love Valley crown, Love Valley being the name for the region where we live, encompassing Sweetkiss Creek, Lake Lorelei, and Taylortown. Unfortunately, though, the jewel has long lost its shine and luster.

"I've been there, but ages ago. I think the last time I was at the campground was when there was an overnight team-building event we did for the fire station, about a year and a half ago."

"It's such a great property, I'm floored that no one's snapped it up. It's got bunkhouses and an RV park. People love it, but what I didn't know about was the number of buildings over there—there are so many stand-alones! And all of them can be used in some way. There's a block of small spaces we're looking at renovating to put retail stores in, so we can make that campground more than just a place for tourists or enthusiasts, but a destination for anyone."

Searching my memory banks, I can recall seeing several buildings around the campground, but I also remember some of them being dilapidated. But who am I to yuck someone else's yum? "I had no idea, but it sounds so promising!"

"Right? It's crazy." Amelia's phone suddenly goes off. She pulls it from her pocket, then glances at it before tucking it back into her pocket. "Oh man. That's my cue, or some people call him Spencer. Time to go and do some work."

Putting her fingers in her mouth, she proceeds to do one of those whistles that are so epic and ear shattering that you either love it or you hate it. Me? I'm in awe.

Barney flies back to her side, with Max hot on his heels, the pair skidding to a stop in front of us, panting. "Looks like Max made a new friend today."

Amelia smiles. "Maybe I did, too. It was nice meeting you."

"You, too. I'll see you at your gallery opening tomorrow night."

With a wave, she jogs back to her car. Max beside me, he waits for them to go before he hops off the bench and takes off, back to business around the park once again.

I stay on the bench for about thirty minutes after Amelia leaves, finally calling Max back to my side when the chill of the sun going down gets to me and I find myself regretting my choice to not bring a jacket. Snapping his leash on his collar, I lead him out of the park and back to the parking lot as a small Volkswagen Beetle comes careening down the driveway and pulls into the spot beside mine.

Behind the wheel waving furiously in my direction is Etta. But it's not Etta who gets my attention, it's the guy beside her that piques my interest. I watch as she opens her driver's side door and gets out, opening the back door to reveal two small schnauzers, who beeline it down the hill, side by side—like conjoined twins who can't do anything alone. I feel like that with Reid sometimes, connected at the hip.

But not today.

"Hey." Reid's head pops up on the other side of the car as he gets out of the passenger side. "I didn't know you'd be here."

"It's not like we check in every day." Actually we do, but today we didn't. Semantics. I nod at Etta. "What are you two doing here?"

"Reid mentioned the dog park had opened, so I convinced him to show me where it was."

"Ahhh." The dog park is not something that would normally be on his radar, but it would be because of Max. And because I told him about it.

"You talked my ear off about it at dinner last night, remember?"

He's right. I did talk his ear off about it and how excited I was to take Max today. It's the little things that make me happy.

"Oh, true." Pulling my keys out, I click the fob to unlock the doors. "Well, it's an amazing park. There's a small pack of Westies that just got here, and one was the same size as your dogs."

"Where have they gone?" Etta stands with hands on her hips, looking around. "Thor, Hercules! Come!"

Sneaking a glance at Reid, it's comical to find him standing in place with a confused look on his face. He looks my way, then starts to lean in to tell me something, but he's blindsided by a schnauzer who's appeared out of nowhere and managed to run smack into his leg.

"Watch it, Thor." I'm not sure why, but Etta clips a leash on the mighty Thor's collar and does the same to the one called Hercules. "I'll take them down to that fenced-in part so they can start running around in safety. See you later, Dylan."

Etta walks away, but a few steps on and a feeling of a taut line hitting the backs of my knees gives me a start. The line is almost pushing me forward, while Max—who is also attached to his leash—is pulling me to the left, toward the car. He's heard me say we're going home, so he's ready.

I've no time to react when my balance is thrown off-kilter on the dusty hillside parking lot. Looking down at my legs, I quickly assess that Etta's leashes...that's right folks, not one but both of 'em...are wrapped around my legs. With each step she takes with Thor and Hercules, I'm pulled like some kind of freakshow-like puppet trying to make its way through an obstacle course with them.

Meanwhile, my torso is being tugged on and directed by Max, who just wants a treat from the center console, for the love of all things furry.

My eyes slam into Reid's as a familiar feeling of weightlessness occurs, and I'm treated to seeing my feet fly in the air in front of my face as I land, hard, on my back in a pile of dust and grass.

I keep my eyes pinched closed, cursing my very existence. Squinting, I open one and find five faces—two human and three canine—all looking down at where I'm laid out on the ground.

"Oh, my gosh!" Etta's face goes white with horror as she

looks at the scene, pointing to the leashes. "This is all my fault. I am so sorry! Why did I hook them back up to their leashes?"

My thoughts, too, but I hurt too badly to even argue. About anything. I think I have a skid mark on my butt where I scraped it on impact.

Gentle hands reach down, arms envelop around me, and help me up. I crane my neck, trying to make sure it's Reid, and can tell it is when I recognize the small tattoo on the inside of his wrist.

He helps steady me, holding on to one of my arms for good measure and to Max's leash as well. "That was a harder fall than you had at the bat house the other night."

I touch the knot on my forehead that is slowly starting to fade. The pain in my butt is incomparable. "You've got that right."

Within a few minutes, I'm feeling better, enough so that I wave goodbye and head to my car, ready to leave and get out of here. I've made enough of a fool out of myself for the time being, may as well save some for later.

Crawling behind the wheel, I watch Etta and Reid walk side by side down to the fenced-in area for small dogs and my heart goes boom. He opens the fence door for her, letting her and her terrorist dogs in with her, pausing as he closes the gate to look in my direction and wave.

Weakly, I lift a hand and return the gesture. It was inevitable that I would fall for you, Reid Shannon. You are kind, you are strong, and you are the most gentle man I've ever met, aside from my father that is.

But, watching him sit down on a bench beside Etta, my mind shifts. Maybe the inevitable is that Reid and Etta are meant for each other, and me? I'll just be in the way.

Maybe.

SEVEN

Reid

Moving will never be one of those tasks one can enjoy, which is why I made it a rule recently that the next time I move, I will hire movers to do all the work for me. Gone are the days of asking my friends if they can help or looking for a truck to borrow for a day, or even trying to rent a U-Haul. No way. As a grown-up, I've made a promise to myself that when I leave this house, I will hire people to get me outta here.

"Your arms really feel it after a few hours of unloading box after box, am I right?"

Zac, my new roommate, stands beside his cousin's old Ford pickup, grinning.

Reaching into the bed of the truck, I stack two of the heavier boxes on top of each other and lift them, gritting my teeth as I smile. "Nah. I'm good."

I don't have to turn around to know Zac's watching me strain as I walk across the lawn and up the steps to the porch. There's no way I can admit to Zac I may have bitten off more than I can chew when I picked up these two boxes. No way, no how.

My arms are actually shaking at this point. Doesn't help that I did a huge arm workout yesterday. My biceps need time to recover, precious time they won't get at this rate.

I silently thank the gods and goddesses around me when I realize I left the front screen door propped open. There's no way I'd be able to put these babies down and pick them back up again.

Most folks would just admit to their friend they can't do something, right? Like, if I was a sane man, I'd put the boxes down, have a laugh with Zac that they *are* a bit heavy, then I'd take them inside one at a time.

But...there's no way on this earth I'm going to do that. That's like pulling over and asking for directions when I'm lost. It's on the list of things I just won't do.

When I met Zac, we got along instantly from the sheer force of our need to compete against one another. I can't explain it—a case of friendly rivalry? Something to ponder as I hike the boxes to his room, plop them down gratefully on his bed, and walk into the kitchen. Grabbing a couple of cold drinks from the fridge, I head back outside, finding Zac on a self-appointed break and sitting on the tailgate of his truck.

"Here." I toss a cold can of Cheerwine in his direction. "I'd give you a beer, but I feel like that's going to be your treat for getting this moving done today. Do you not have any other friends or family who can help you move? I mean, we both know if anyone can afford to hire movers, you can, Zac."

It's true. Zac comes from the Wright family, one of the founding families in South Carolina. The thing I thought was cool about him was that when I met him, he wasn't the kind of guy who threw all of his money and prestige in your face. No, he's the kind of guy who borrows his cousin's truck to move.

"Nope, it's just me." Zac cracks open his can of soda and takes a swig. "My dad couldn't get away and my mom is in

Canada visiting her sister. Sadly, I couldn't rally anyone to help, not even my little sister. She's working for the Beaufort Fire Department now and couldn't get time off."

I sip my soda and lean against the truck bed. "Is she a volunteer, like you?"

Zac shakes his head. "Full time. She loves it."

"One kid is a cop, the other in the fire department." I raise my can in the air. "The Wright family makes the rest of us look like mere mortals."

"Ha." Zac swipes at me, but I manage to sidestep his swing. "Being the local cop in Sweetkiss Creek is hardly the stuff superheroes are made of. But I'm looking forward to it."

"Oh, you'll see plenty of action in good ole Sweetkiss." No, he really won't, but I don't mind telling this little lie. "There's Jon Tucker, he's the local dance instructor and likes to do those pop-up things. I forget what they're called..."

Zac's eyes light up. "Flash mobs?"

I snap my fingers. "That's it! A flash mob. He puts one together, like, every week. Finds a reason to surprise someone with a dance number. It's not that big of a population, so you'd think he would run out of people to do it by now."

"Still going?" Zac asks before he takes another sip of his drink.

Taking a long slow sip of my drink, I swallow before I answer. "Still goin'."

Pushing myself off the back of the truck, I'm about to suggest we grab the last few boxes when the sound of tires crunching on gravel gets my attention. The very sight of her takes me back to our dinner out and the hot sauce that was on her lips, smeared all over them. Everything about that shouldn't be so sexy to me, but it's not about the sauce, it's about those lips. Those perfect, kissable lips that I've stared at whenever I've had the chance over the last two years.

Can I help it that the sauce made my mouth water,

making me feel like a feral animal who wanted to nibble those lips? Those luscious, provocative lips, which are parted now and glistening as she smiles and waves at us from behind the wheel of her car.

Dylan pulls in the drive, Max sitting at her side with his mouth open and tongue wagging. She no sooner opens her car door when Max comes flying out and running up to greet me.

"Maxie!" Bending over, I scratch my favorite furry bundle of happiness between the ears. "How's my little man?"

"On his way to the vet, but shush, don't let him know that."

My hand brushes hers as she also leans down to pet his head, and an electric current races through me. Is vet talk a fetish? "Is he going for a checkup?"

"Yeah, time for his yearly shots."

Glancing up, I'm hit with how beautiful Dylan looks today. Her hair is pulled up loosely into a bun on top of her head, her cheeks flush a shade of pink that shows off her features, while the pleated skirt she chose to wear today highlights her legs. Legs that go for miles, if not days.

Wow.

I gather myself quickly, standing erect and trying not to look at her like a hungry wolf, because that's exactly how I feel right now. I scoop Max into my arms to keep myself busy and fight the rush of nervousness that's hitting my veins suddenly. I even touch my mouth just to make sure my tongue isn't wagging.

"So." Dylan's eyes graze across mine but flick to take in Zac on my right-hand side. "Are you going to introduce me?"

"Oh, sorry." Propping Max in my arms, I do things properly. "Dylan, this is Zac. Old friend from Beaufort who lives here now."

Zac holds his hand out to shake Dylan's. But he holds it for a beat longer than I would like, that's for sure.

"Nice to meet you." Does he have to smile at her like that? "You're Dubs's daughter, right?"

"Have you done your research?" Don't think I don't notice when Dylan's tone turns flirtatious. "Can't imagine you two know each other, or I would have heard."

"Dubs is a legend in Beaufort. I'm a volunteer at the station there, but my dad and sister are full time."

"Dubs is a legend?" Dylan crosses her arms in front of her chest, smiling. "That's sweet to know."

Not sure why, but my skin prickles. Pretty sure if I was a dog, my hackles would be raised. And they'd be hackley. There is something in this exchange I don't like. My eyes rock back and forth, watching Dylan and Zac as they chat easily, but mostly I'm watching Zac.

And I've seen that look in his eyes before.

"I just came by to drop this back to you." Dylan hands me my jacket. "I got home after dinner the other night and realized I still had it. Sorry about that."

"No worry at all." I'm aiming for nonchalant as I take it from her and throw it on the truck bed like it's nothing. The best part is knowing when I put that jacket on, I'll be treated to a whiff of her perfume. Jasmine and sweet pea, so subtle and so good. "Thanks for bringing it back."

Dylan grins in my direction and points to Max, who is still chilling out in my arms and soaking up the pats I'm giving him. "May I have him back? Our appointment is in ten minutes, so we gotta go."

"Bye, buddy." I kiss the little guy's head and hand him back over to his owner's waiting arms. "Talk to you later?"

"Maybe I'll see you at the gallery tonight?"

Is that hope in her voice? I think I just hope there's hope.

"Maybe." I walk over to her car and lean closer to her window so only she can hear me. "Gotta see how this goes. If I have energy after we get done, I'll be there."

"Cool." Her eyes flick back over to Zac before she meets mine again. "He seems nice. You two have fun."

And with a wave, she's gone. I haven't had the chance to even turn around before Zac starts asking me questions.

"Wowzer." First, he whistles. Low, slow, and a little too long for my taste. "Is she single?"

My jaw tightens. "She is."

"So not dating anyone special. Right?"

I can't lie and say she is when she isn't. "Not that I'm aware of."

Zac grins, his eyes boring into me. My nerves are firing up and I'm starting to feel a little nauseated when my phone rings in my back pocket.

Grateful for the interruption, I grab it and press the button to say hello without looking at the screen to see who it is.

"Are you free?" It's Etta. "I've got the chance to go see a storefront in Sweetkiss Creek where I could put my tasting room. I need a second opinion and was hoping I could have yours?"

Stepping away from the insanity of moving would be a nice reprieve, and Zac only has a few boxes left to move anyway, but it also means I'd be walking away from these uncomfortable questions he keeps asking me about Dylan.

"Sure. Give me the address and I'll see you there."

———

Back in the car already, I point us in the direction for Lake Lorelei, while beside me, Etta shakes her head as she flips through the paperwork the realtor gave her.

"Well, that's a bummer. How can anyone charge such a high price for rent and not even be on the main street in town?" She shuffles the papers for a moment longer before tossing them to the floor by her feet. "I mean, seriously! The whole place needs to be repainted and have new flooring put in, and I would have to do it as part of the agreement, plus pay for rent on top of it? No way. Dreaming."

"Hey, you gave it a look and now you know. The realtor did say if it's out of your price range to let her know what you're looking for and she could help you."

"I don't know. I feel like she wants a nice commission and to put me where the prices are higher, but I'm looking for inexpensive. A cozy little spot for a tasting room, nothing extravagant. Homey and classy, which makes no sense, but I know the crowd I want to attract."

"You sound like you know what you want. Like Dylan always says to me, listen to your gut. If it's telling you no, then don't do it." Slowing down for a stop light, I turn my head so I'm facing Etta, who's watching me with a funny look on her face.

"You two are pretty close, huh?"

If by pretty close, she means I think about Dylan all the time, then yes. We are as close as two pieces of Velcro.

"We're tight. We spend a lot of time together because of work. But like what you said about the realtor trying to talk you into it, she's the same way. She can't stand it when the people around her try to 'upsell' her, as she likes to say."

"I get it. I want what I want, not what they think I want." Etta laughs when she finishes her sentence. "Apparently, I'm related to Dr. Seuss."

"I like the *Cat in the Hat*." The light turns green and I press on the gas, keeping us on our path. "I think *Cat in the Hat* was my first taste of what cool art could look like."

"Speaking of art, are you going to that exhibition that's opening tonight at Gallery on the Creek?"

I mean, I wasn't *not* planning on going, but I wasn't sure. Since I had to write about the upcoming exhibit, I've already been treated to a special preview, so I've actually seen the exhibition in its entirety. It's a fun one, but not one I'd planned on going back to any time soon.

But, Dylan is going. That I know.

Even though my heart does its flippity thing when I think about Dylan, I play things off very nonchalantly. "I've been thinking about it. I may see if Zac feels up to it, since it's his first day here and all."

"Bring him, too. If you want to come, that is."

One thing for sure, there's another vibe happening right now. I feel like I'm being pulled into some kind of weird vortex—is Etta trying to oh-so-subtly ask me to meet her there?

This is a no-no place, and for many reasons. Part of me screams to retreat, but another part of me sees a way out. In fact, it could be a way to essentially kill two birds with one stone.

"You know what? I think I will go tonight." Hitting the blinker, I merge the car onto Main Street in Lake Lorelei.

"Yeah?" Etta's voice goes up at the end of the word, proving that hope floats.

"Why not? I'm sure Zac will be into it."

Etta claps her hands together. "Oh that's so fun! I love that I'll know people at this event."

I feel kind of bad, knowing that I'm going only for the sheer fact that my own kind of hope is floating at this moment. Is it so awful that I want Etta to turn Zac's head so he'll pay attention to her and forget about Dylan?

Fingers. Crossed.

EIGHT

Dylan

I've been staring at myself in the mirror for the last half hour, checking and rechecking the bare existence of makeup I managed to slap on my face. I used to love getting up in the morning and getting ready for work when I worked as an event planner in L.A., but these days, I'm more inclined to go with the minimal amount of anything I can get away with.

Max snores quietly at my feet, snuggled into the white fluffy rug beneath me. I bend over, being careful so I don't disturb him, and pull my makeup kit out from under the sink. I feel like taking it up a notch tonight, so why not?

Within twenty minutes, I have blended my foundation, added more highlighter to my cheeks, applied my favorite color of lipstick, and I'm standing with my mascara wand in hand when my cell phone makes a loud chime at the same time that my doorbell rings.

Startled by the sudden activity, Max leaps up and tears down the hall to the front door, barking.

"Hang on." Grabbing my phone, I take a look at the screen as I jog to the door.

RILEY: HEY! I'M BEHIND, LIKE USUAL. MEET YOU AND ETTA AT THE GALLERY.

I manage to step around Max, who is going insane not out of want for being a guard dog, but because it's his job to bark and that's all he knows how to do. I don't think if anyone ever came along and decided to break into my place, Max would be the best dog to be on the job. He loves treats and would throw me under a bus to get one.

Throwing the door open, it's no surprise after Riley's text to find Etta standing there solo.

"Hey." She raises a hand and drops it, awkwardly. "I guess Riley texted you by now?"

I wave my phone in the air. "Just got it. Wanna come in?"

Etta steps inside, looking around the small living room. "Is Dubs here? I was hoping to say hi."

"No, he's on duty tonight."

You know when a friendship is new, and you're in a room with this person who you kind of know, yet you're still figuring each other out...and it's just kinda uncomfortable?

Yeah. Well, this moment is like that. On steroids. I can tell Etta would have liked to have someone else around to buffer us as much as I do, so now I feel like I must remove myself from the room so we can both get a second.

Inclining my head in the direction of the hallway, I plaster on my brightest smile. "I'm going to finish up in the bathroom. Help yourself to anything in the kitchen. I'll be right back."

I head back down to the bathroom to finish my mascara, grateful for the moment to myself. I may take a few extra seconds too long on my lashes, but I'm with Etta in the kitchen within five minutes.

Etta stands with her back to me, holding a beer in one hand and Max in the other. She's standing close to the refrigerator, looking at the photos I have plastered across it, all secured for viewing pleasure by old magnets. Magnets that tell the tale of any vacation Dad or I have ever gone on, because whenever we leave, we make it a rule we come back with a magnet that reflects where we've been.

Etta points to one photo of Dad and me standing next to a giant donut. "Is that here in Lake Lorelei somewhere?"

"Actually, that one was taken in Los Angeles." I tap the magnet emblazoned with L.A. across it. "Each magnet coincides with the photo so we can remember where we were when it was taken."

Etta's eyes light up. "That's a great idea!" She leans in closer, inspecting the fridge once again, and points to one of Reid and me in our gear standing in a parking lot, but the magnet is a giant peach. "I'm going to guess this was in Georgia?"

"Yeah, the peach gives it away." Chuckling, I excuse myself and open the door to the fridge, plucking a bottle of water from inside before closing it shut. "We were there for a week of training; I think your brother actually took that one."

Smiling, I lean forward and move a giant blue crab magnet off another photo so I can show it to Etta. "This one is my favorite. Reid and I went to work in Baltimore, Maryland for a month to help out when they were low on staff. Have you ever had steamed crabs?"

I pass the photo to Etta, who starts laughing. The photo shows Reid wearing a giant bib around his neck and sitting at a picnic table lined with brown paper. On top of the paper a bushel of steamed crabs has been dumped out and he's sitting there, holding a mallet in one hand and a tiny picking fork in the other with a goofy grin on his face. On top of his head loosely sits a giant paper chef's hat that one of the guys had made for him in a quick DIY fashion, writing "Reid's got crabs!" across it.

"Wow." She chuckles, setting Max back on the ground. "He lets you keep this photo up of him?"

"He does." My heart skips a tiny beat thinking about that trip. It was only last year that we'd gone and we'd had so much fun. When we weren't at the station, we were being taken out on boats to go fishing in the Chesapeake Bay or exploring the nearby towns. One night we'd even managed to sneak into a baseball game, getting to see the Baltimore Orioles play against the New York Yankees. "We had the best time together on that trip."

Slowly, Etta turns to face me, smiling. "I can tell you two have been friends for a long time...haven't you?"

"Since I moved here—" Suddenly, my doorbell chimes. Cocking my head to the side, I look at Etta and hold up one finger. "Hold up. Let me see who that is. Maybe Riley changed her mind."

I'm in front of the door in a few strides, surprised to find Amelia in front of me clutching a bouquet of flowers.

"How did you know where I live?"

"And hello to you, too." Amelia laughs. Her laughter tinkles, filling the air like a tiny bell would. A tiny bell attached to a gorgeous fairy. "You mentioned you worked for your dad's garage, and seeing as there are only two car garages in the area, I figured one of them would know who you were." She grins and taps her head. "Deductive reasoning."

"So, you thought you'd bring me flowers?"

"Oh, no." She looks down at the bouquet in her hand. "I was in the area to pick these up. My husband, bless his heart, ordered them for tonight, but I asked him to order them from The Watering Can. It's in Sweetkiss Creek and a five-minute walk from the shop." She holds up the massive bundle. "He ordered them from Crazy Daisy's, the new florist on the other side of Lake Lorelei. I was actually really frustrated and a bit irritated with him to go back to work, so I was hoping to hang out with you and maybe have a cup of tea and calm down first."

"Lucky for you, I have a plethora of decaf tea in my cabinet." Another bonus present from Reid a few months ago. I swear, mention to that guy you're battling anything, like I did when I told him how I was getting anxious, and he shows up with ways to help. Like a knight in shining armor, who always knows when to appear by your side.

I usher Amelia inside and introduce her to Etta, who's found her way out of the kitchen and has joined us in the living room. Leaving them alone to chat, I duck into the kitchen and fire up my tea kettle. Within minutes, I'm back in the room to find Etta and Amelia chatting away.

"So they were charging how much for that space?" Amelia shakes her head in disbelief. "It's not even in a prime location, in my opinion. You'd be off the main road, so there would hardly be any walking traffic."

"I know. And I want to be somewhere that people will see it, but also somewhere that will aid in keeping the vibe lively, you know? Being set off the beaten track does not instill confidence in me that I'd get the right clientele in there, if I had anyone come in at all."

"I'm sure you'd have folks find you, but you'll have to ramp up your marketing efforts." I hand Amelia her drink and take a seat beside her on the couch, facing Etta who is sitting across from us, in Dad's favorite chair. "One way to cement your status when you get in your store is to have a launch party that will knock everyone's socks off, right?"

"Ohhh. True!" Etta's eyes light up. "I love parties."

"Me, too." Amelia holds up her mug, toasting nothing in particular. "Thank you for this. I swear, marriage is not for the faint of heart. I love my husband—LOVE—but some days, I require an epic amount of patience so I don't say the wrong thing."

Swiping the water bottle off the coffee table, I take a swig as I watch Amelia. I know people well enough to know that sometimes their words may be playful, but the hurt in her eyes tells me there's more.

However, Etta and her one-way brain don't get that memo. "Now I'm wondering if I said no to that place too fast. Maybe I can go back and look at it and consider a bigger marketing campaign."

Amelia tilts her head to one side before honing in on Etta. "But why do that when your gut told you not to get it the first time you were there?"

I nod, agreeing. "She has a point. I don't know about you guys, but when it comes to my gut, I've learned to listen to it. If you didn't feel the vibe you wanted from that place, Etta, you can't make it work now because of marketing. You won't be happy there no matter what."

Suddenly a lightbulb goes off over my head. If this was a cartoon, it would literally have appeared: a tiny lightbulb graphic, sliding onto the TV screen out of nowhere, turning on bright yellow to signal to the world that "I've got an idea!"

"Amelia, didn't you say there was some possible space for lease at the Sweetkiss Creek campground? Like, spaces you were thinking of putting retail shops in for your guests?" I turn and look at Etta, who is busy pulling her mass of strawberry blonde hair back into a secure bun, and I shrug my shoulders. "I mean, you could check it out."

"A tasting room in a campground?" Etta looks at me like I've spent too long in a wine barrel myself. "Wouldn't that be odd?

"Not necessarily." The corner of Amelia's mouth twitches with what I can only describe as delight. "In fact, this could be a cool draw to have as part of the campground. An actual tasting room with a wine aficionado who is on site to answer questions? How cool would that be!"

"We could plan special packages." Etta's speech is fast now, excited. "Encourage groups to come and stay, but I can plan out wine packages for them or tasting parties. Ohhh, maybe I should carry cheese, too?"

"Now we're talking!" Amelia claps her hands together and looks at her watch. "Oh boy, I need to get back. Spencer will be wondering where I am. I told him I'd be back by now, but to be fair...he put me in a position where I needed to get my passport out just to go pick up a bouquet of flowers."

"Completely understand." Giggling, I hop up and grab my car keys and look at Etta. "We're right behind you."

As we all file out the front door and spill onto the drive, Amelia skips ahead, turning back and pointing a finger at Etta.

"Let's talk in a few days, okay? I'll get your number at the gallery and we'll go from there."

With a flick of her wrist to wave goodbye, Ameila is gone as fast as she appeared. I watch her until she's out of sight, then turn to Etta standing beside me, looking disheveled but optimistic.

"Wow. She's a hurricane. But in disguise." She shakes her head, laughing. "I mean, a tasting room. On a campground? Who would have thought it? It's just so crazy it might work."

NINE

Reid

L ooking around the tiny gallery, I feel happily
responsible for its capacity. It's busy, stuffed full of
people who were standing outside in a long line to get
in, and well before the doors even opened. According to
Amelia, who had flown past Zac and me a few moments prior,
the majority of them had found out about the opening from
Andrew's column.

So am I taking this as a personal win? You bet I am.

I'd arrived about thirty minutes ago with Zac, waiting to
enter a few minutes after the doors had opened...can't risk
looking too eager. But I want to be here before Dylan arrives.

The paper had made an agreement with Amelia to keep
my identity a secret, so I'd had the chance already to walk
through the gallery as part of the write-up—and I'm thankful
I was able to come in alone. I'm also feeling a little weird
because, once again, I'm slinking around in the shadows
writing up stories as an anonymous person. Yet, I'm meeting
the people behind the businesses as Reid and, in some cases,
becoming friendly with them. It all feels a bit weird, but what
I write is well received, so I need to stop overthinking things.

Putting my own insecurities on a backburner, I take in the gallery, which has morphed from the brightly lit studio it is during the day to a sexy, sultry and vibey spot for the night. The walls are lined with pieces of art placed in clean lines for the eye to take in, on canvases of all sizes. The showing tonight is for a local pop artist who has been studying in New York and Paris. She's finally come home to show off her works here before she leaves for California.

Looking around the room, I see the artist, who goes only by her first name, Tiara. She's huddled in a corner with her agent and Amelia, hopefully toasting their success. I'd spent a lot of time talking to her on the phone for our interview, and I have to admit, I'm a little jealous. She's gone off and really attacked her dream with passion.

Amelia must have felt my eyes boring a hole in her back. She turns around and gives me a half-wave. I wave my hello and turn away, only to find Zac standing and staring at me, his eyes bouncing back and forth between Tiara, Amelia, and me with a dopey grin on his face.

"So, did you want to get here early for the hot blonde over there?"

Rolling my eyes, I slug his arm. "Shut up, man. That's the owner, who is married. You should be getting to know people here on a more personal level, since you're going to be policing the area for them."

Silently I pat myself on the back for the redirect. I've gotten good at hiding my identity over the past year. I mean, it's not like I'm Batman; I'm writing a culture blog basically, even though Dylan would argue—on Andrew's behalf—it's a column, but still. Being anonymous and able to write my opinion is freeing.

Beside me, Zac nods his head, agreeing with me. "You know what? You're right." He stands up a little taller and straightens his button-down shirt, tucking it in a little tighter.

"I'm going to make more of an effort to start getting to know the good people of Sweetkiss Creek."

Narrowing my eyes, I look him up and down. "It's not the old west, nor are we in an episode of Yellowstone. Just mingle. The people around here are laid-back and good, but it is a tight-knit community."

"I like a town like that. One where I can really trust the folks in it, where I'll feel comfortable." Zac nods, his eyes drawn to something over my shoulder. "I'm looking forward to getting to know the very good people of both Sweetkiss Creek and Lake Lorelei very, very much. I think I should start now, don't you?"

When Zac walks away, it's his use of all those verys that prompts me to spin around to see what he had been looking at. By the time I've turned around, he's standing in front of a trio of women, all smiling and laughing and saying hello. Right in the very center of the throng is the only reason I'm here tonight.

Very interesting.

Why is it that only recently my heart started dropping outside of my chest and landing square in my hands whenever I see Dylan? And tonight, she is breathtaking. Her hair is pulled up on top of her head, piled into a bun, and she's even tucked a few rosebuds in it, giving her an ethereal effect. She looks over and, on seeing me, dare I even think her face lights up when she's waving?

If anyone knows me inside and out, besides my sister that is, it's this woman. Since we met I have had no choice but to be unapologetically myself with her. I know it sounds sad, but I've never had anyone around me that I could do that with. At least not of the female persuasion. I've got great guy friends, my family...but the couple of girlfriends I had over the years had been non-starters. One only wanted to be with me because I'm a fireman. Shocker. It happens. But the other—a classmate at school—had stung. Things had fallen apart when I found out she had been cheating on me.

I was young, but it had cut deep. I come from a family where we don't cheat. Heck, we don't do lies. The fact I'm keeping the Andrew secret from my family is bad enough. And yes, that's the most risqué my life gets and I am one hundred percent a-okay with it.

But these days, Dylan is my anchor, only she doesn't know it. I know things are going to be okay because I have her in my corner. Seeing her smile calms me, and when she breaks away from the group she's standing with and makes a beeline for where I am, my heart pounds like a bass drum in my chest.

"Hey." She wraps an arm around me as she leans in for a quick hug. "How's it going with the new roommate?"

Across the room, Zac is busy entertaining Riley, who seems to be hanging on to his every word.

"Good...so far." I lift a shoulder and let it drop. "But the night is young. The Zac I remember is a good guy but can be a little too much sometimes."

"Too much?" Dylan's eyebrow quirks, and my heart skips. "Like what?"

"Overeager? Excited?" I'm laughing now, mostly because Dylan's face is twisted in pure confusion. "Look, he always means well, but he's just super passionate when he's into something."

"I love it when someone's passion is so big and so intense that they take you on the journey with them." Dylan's eyes flick to mine, candlelight dancing in their reflection. "Passion can be underrated, you know."

Am I staring at Dylan's parted lips, waiting to hear what falls out of them next? You bet I am.

"Passion is a big emotion. One must be careful when labeling something as passionate, since it means a strong and barely controllable emotion."

Who do I think I am? Reid Oxford Dictionary? Dylan breaks into laughter and reaches out and grabs my arm. Her very touch feels like I've walked into a room that's been on fire for days and the embers are still glowing bright. Shivering, I stare at where her hand rests before dragging my eyes back to meet hers.

This is the moment I should open my mouth and say something. The room is filled to the brim with people, but I only see her, and from the look she's giving me, I swear I think she is feeling the same thing. I want to tell her she doesn't need to worry about finding a place to live, or about her dad. I want to tell her it's going to be okay because I need it to be okay. I don't want her to ever not be here. With me. Beside me. Near me.

As perspiration hits my palms, the realization that I have fallen in love with my best friend hits me and hits me hard. Like a giant steel wall has slammed against me and forced me backwards, it's intense. It's uncontrollable. It's...passion.

"Hate to break this up, but we can't stay too long." Out of what feels like nowhere, Riley has slipped in beside Dylan and brought Zac and Etta with her. "We have reservations at the sushi restaurant we need to get to soon."

"I love sushi," Zac pipes in. His eyes bounce between Etta and Dylan. "One of the hardest things about moving is having to find new places, like restaurants you like."

"I'm sure you can get someone to taste test some places with you." Clearly uninterested in Zac's fishing for an invite to their dinner out, Riley's voice trails off as she spots Amelia and waves. "I'm going to go say hi to Amelia and then I'll meet you guys outside in, like, twenty minutes?"

Dylan and Etta both nod simultaneously, and we all watch her trot off, leaving the four of us staring at each other. Instinct has me wanting to wrap my arms around Dylan or at least sidle over closer to her, maybe rub myself on her so I can put a scent on her that will turn anyone (Zac) and everyone else (again, mostly Zac) off.

"She's right, you know." Etta crosses her arms and tilts her head to one side, turning to Zac. "Reid introduced me to my favorite Mexican joint, and that's in Taylortown. And I found my favorite Thai restaurant the other day when I was out looking at houses, and that's here in Sweetkiss Creek."

"I'm not so much a fan of Thai food." Zac shrugs, brushing Etta off but keeping his eyes trained on Dylan. "What about you, Dylan?"

"I love pad thai." Dylan smiles and tosses a hand in the air. "It's my comfort food of choice."

"You can't beat a good red curry." Etta bobs her head in agreement, eyeing me. "Hold on. Didn't you tell me there's a new Thai place opening soon? Somewhere around here."

"Yep." Andrew had been invited to the opening of Tuk Tuk Thai, a new place opening in Sweetkiss Creek in a few days, but Reid had not. Had I told Etta this when I had my guard down? I'm usually pretty good at keeping my knowledge of cool things to do separate. Those insights are reserved for my alter ego, thank you very much. "I think I overheard it at the gym the other day, but yes, it opens soon."

"We should go." I look over at Zac, thinking he's suggesting all four of us go out to dinner, but he's focused solely on Dylan, who wriggles uncomfortably where she stands as he waits for her answer. "Maybe you can teach me a thing or two about Thai food, convince me to like it more than I do?"

Dylan never likes to be put on the spot, and Mr. Overexcited has managed to accidentally tickle her anxiety button. I know that her anxiety has been at an epic peak recently, and I know with everything her dad is dealing with, this interaction with Zac could only heighten her senses. After hesitating, she finally opens her mouth to answer when I make my move.

"That's a great idea!" Slapping Zac on the back, I throw my arm around his neck to add some levity to the situation. "Why don't all four of us go on a date to the new Thai place? Think of something else to do after?" Turning my attention to Dylan, I touch her arm. My way of letting her know I've got this now. "Maybe we can make it an active date, less talking."

"You're brilliant." Dylan's eyes light up and she nods her head in unison with mine. "Love that idea!" She turns to Etta and nudges her arm. "You in?"

Beaming, Etta grins and her head bobs up and down in agreement. "You bet."

Pulling her eyes from mine, after mouthing a silent thank you my way, Dylan looks at her watch. "We have ten minutes left before Riley wants us to get outta here and go eat." Pointing her thumb over her shoulder, she winks at me. "I'm going to go see what I can see before we leave. Talk to you tomorrow?"

"We have a shift together tomorrow, so try not to." It sounded cooler in my head, but when it comes out of my mouth, I feel like a dad trying to make a joke but failing miserably.

Leave it to Dylan, she gets me. She pinches her lips and rolls her eyes, fighting a laugh before she gives me a last wave. She disappears into the throng of people behind Etta, leaving me with a sole wish that she was my date for the night, not the guy beside me.

I can still make out the top of her head as they weave through the crowd, heading for the front door. As she slips away, a feeling knocks on my heart as realization slams inside me.

I don't ever want to let her go.

TEN

"Do you know if anyone makes a perfume that blends the smells of ink and fresh newspaper, backed with the scent of a pot of coffee that's been brewed only moments ago but also sprinkled with some grease?"

I close my eyes and take another whiff of the Sunday newspaper in my father's hands before leaning back into my own chair and breathing out. "Heaven."

My dad sips his coffee, used to my antics. "Between this and the fact you enjoy the smell of gas, I should really wonder about you."

"Rubber glue and markers. I love the smell of those, too." Winking, I point to the jelly container in front of my dad's plate. "Can you slide some of that strawberry jelly this way? My toast is sad without it."

Two grunts and a "shhh" later, Dad is back, nosed pressed into the national section of the *Lake Lorelei News Post*. This is our routine on Sundays, or at least it has been since I moved here. I love that we always manage to make time to spend our Sunday mornings with each other.

When I look around the dining room of the small cafe, I see people I've come to know and love over the past two years. There's the Kline family in the corner—we actually rescued their son and their cat from their front yard magnolia recently. The cat climbed up, so little Timmy did, too. Little Timmy also stuffed pussy willows up his nose last year, which Reid had the pleasure of extracting in the back of the ambulance. Little Timmy is a frequent flier, you could say. He also likes to think he is an actual cat, relying on a meow to get his point across sometimes...hmm. I'm starting to understand why he went up that tree.

Then there's the Harkness clan. Super nice transplants who came to live in North Carolina after living in Arizona forever. They pretty much keep to themselves—he loves to talk about the news or dig into some kind of existential conversation about where the world is headed, and she's the kind of woman you can chat about anything with, but bring up Bravo and kiss the next thirty minutes of your life goodbye. Their kids are all in college as of this year, but each holiday all six are back and usually causing chaos at home. Last year was the turkey fryer incident, and the year before we helped get one of the kids down off the roof when they were stuck up there after putting up Christmas lights. One brother had gone up to do the actual work, and the other five decided to hide the ladder from him. Those guys. Makes you wonder about having kids sometimes, but hey, their parents still love them.

Scanning the room, my eyes land on Riley, who gives me a wave as she walks over to our table with more coffee.

"Here you go." Riley tips her piping hot carafe into my mug then into Dad's, inclining her head toward the paper in his hands. "Have you read Andrew's column and seen what's opening this week?"

"Aww." I grin her way as I place my coffee cup to my lips. "You said column."

Riley rolls her eyes, sighing. "I meant blog."

"Whatever." We'll never get past this. I hold my hand out to my father. "May I?"

Once again treating me to one of his grunts of displeasure, he rifles through his stack of paper and finds the arts and culture section, handing it over to me. I flip through the pages while Riley peers over my shoulder.

"Did you make sure to go home after the gallery the other night and comment on his post?" she whispers in my ear. "Tell your man you're sooooo thankful he told you about it? That you loooooove art?"

Although I resist her antagonistic barbs, Riley gets me to stop what I'm doing, but only for a second. Then, ignoring her—which I know makes her crazier—I flip on.

"Yes, I did. It's a nice thing to do, to say thank you for telling me and my friends about another cool thing we get to do." Hearing her snort, I turn around and smack the arm that's not holding the hot pot of coffee. "Stop it. I'm telling you, he's the perfect man."

"Shame I can't find out who Andrew is and where he lives, I swear I'd drag you to his door so you could meet him." Riley chuckles in my ear. "Although he's probably got, like, three teeth in his head, one strand of hair that he pulls back into a sorry excuse for a man bun, and likes to build Lego cities in his spare time."

"Be nice." Finding Culture Shock's page, I fold the paper to a more manageable size and quickly scan it. The newest write-up has a breakdown of businesses opening in the area, including Lock and Key, the new escape room.

Pointing to the article, I look up at Riley who is still poised over my shoulder, reading. "This?"

Riley nods. "Those things are supposed to keep your brain busy. Could be a good idea––for you especially." She and Dad make eye contact and share a secret look between them. "You know, since you'll be there watching the man you're into on a date with another woman."

"Or who, apparently, you're simply pushing into his arms?" Dad peers at me over his glasses and gives a shameful shake of his head. "Didn't I raise you better?"

"Wait a second." I drop the paper on the table and throw my hands in the air. "Are you two ganging up on me now?"

Riley shakes her head from side to side and taps on the paper before pointing to my planner, which sits on the table beside me. "We're suggesting you do something that has more action, that's all. So, stick it in that planner of yours and then go home and think about it, okay?"

"Sassy." I reach out and try to slap at her, but she's too quick for me. And luckily Mr. Kline needs more coffee, so she's out of here and making her rounds again, pausing every few seconds to shoot me a look and stick out her tongue.

I turn halfway in my seat, laying my eyes on my father and giving him my best glare. "Being nosy?"

"Being a dad." He sighs. "But some days I feel like I'm failing at that."

Seeing his face darken, I reach over and squeeze his hand. "Hey, we don't get depressed on Sundays."

"It's hard not to think about my situation any day, every day, all day." He tries to smile, but I can see it's forced. "I talked to my sisters back in California and asked if they'd be able to help out since a loan from the bank isn't looking promising."

"Oh?" I try not to sound too excited, but my ears have perked up. I cross my fingers, and my toes for that matter. "Any luck?"

His gaze stays on his plate in front of him "No. Neither one is in a position to co-sign for me, or to loan me anything. They have their own issues right now."

"Being a grown-up is overrated," I sigh.

"So is playing martyr."

My head cranks to the side. "Who's being a martyr?"

My father looks pointedly at me. "The same person who is trying to set up Reid on a date with someone who we all know he's not interested in."

This again. "I'm leaving you and your 'girlfriend' alone. Why can't you guys leave me and my..."

Putting the paper down, a sly grin creeps its way across my dad's face. "And your what? What is he to you, sweetie?"

What is he to me? He's everything, but I can't even form the words. Reid means safety, warmth, and friendship. He's laughter and big hugs that go on for far too long, but are so delicious you want them to go on forever. He's squishy, amazing, hot melted caramel goodness all wrapped up inside a crispy, crunchy exterior that needs a little smoothing. He's my knight in shining armor, only the armor has kinks in it...but, I know how to get them out.

"He's my Reid and there is no one definition for what that means." Redirect, redirect. "Kind of like having you, Daddy. As Sinead O'Connor said, nothing compares to you."

Dad narrows his eyes and takes me in, and I sit and grin at him like the Cheshire cat from *Alice in Wonderland*. "I have one last question for you. Why on earth did you organize this whole date situation?"

"I didn't." I sit up and lean my elbows on the table, grabbing my coffee cup. "Zac was attempting to ask me out, I think. I froze when he did, cause he was asking me out in front of everyone at the gallery." I take a sip of my coffee, then set it back down on the table. "Before I could answer, Reid—or it could have been Etta—chimed in, and I'm not sure from there, but someone suggested we all go out together."

I mean, it is the truth. I started to do a hazy blackout thing when I realized Zac was indeed gearing up to ask me out. You know when you get a tingle up your spine and across your flesh that someone likes you and they're trying to get your attention? I've had that with Zac since the day I met him at Reid's. He seems nice enough, but let's face it. My heart is obviously spoken for, so...no.

"Okay. Just be careful." Dad lifts the paper, disappearing behind the sports section. "Small town, big gossip."

"Is that why you're keeping your little lass a secret still?"

"It is exactly why. Neither one of us needs anyone else talking about our dating life until we're ready for them to have opinions." He winks at me, reaching out to take my hand. "Thank you to you, too, for letting me have that right now. I want you to meet her first, but I want to make sure she's going to be around for a long time before we do that."

The coffee I've just sipped almost sprays from my lips. "It's serious, isn't it?"

Closing the paper, he folds it and tosses it into the chair next to him. "It hurt a lot when your mother left us. A single dad, raising a mini version of myself was awesome, but I was lonely. I poured so much of myself into you, into my work, and now into that garage and the fire station here. It's nice to put attention into myself, what I want, and into Connie..."

"Hold up." Did I hear him right? I turn my head left, then right, then lean over closer and whisper. "Did you...are you... you're dating Connie?"

The crimson flush that creeps from the base of his neck up toward his hairline is all I need to see.

"Oh my—you are. It's Connie!"

"Shush!" I've never seen my dad act like this. I think he may be twitching or he's jerking his head around, and trying to do it subtly, only it looks robotic, like he's a frightened man peeking through his curtains. "We're not ready for anyone to know yet, okay?"

I hold my hands up in surrender and lean away from him. "Okay, but give me a minute to digest this."

I'm not surprised he's dating, but that he's dating Connie? I take a moment to let this one sink in. I've met her. Connie is one of the local dispatchers for the area. I think she's been on the job since she got out of college, and no, I do not know what year it was. She's quite tight-lipped about her age, but she's not so tight-lipped about your business. Everyone lovingly calls her "Le Mouth of le South" because if you don't want someone to know something, you cannot tell her.

Staring at my hands in my lap, I'm fighting the urge to laugh hysterically. Biting down on my lip, I take some deep breaths into my diaphragm and let them out again, slowly, through my nose. Gathering myself, I swallow down a giggle before pulling my eyes up to meet his, hoping I have an air of seriousness now.

"I don't want to go on about it, but let me ask you this." I hold one finger in the air. "How?"

"I can't explain, Dyls. It just happened." Sheepishly, he grins while also initiating the nickname he's had for me since I was a little girl. "I've known Connie since I moved here, and it feels like forever. We've always gotten along. It's the strangest thing, you know. I—we—have always existed together in this little ecosystem here, working side by side, and one day I was at headquarters filing some paperwork when I looked over and saw her sitting there."

"Saw her?"

"Like, I *saw* her." He smiles. "She was eating a chicken sandwich and a hunk of lettuce fell out of the wrapper."

My lack of poker face in this moment reflects my horror, I'm sure. "You fell for her with a piece of wet lettuce hanging out of her mouth? Does she know this?"

"It wasn't that, silly." He shakes his head. "It's the laugh that came out of her when it happened. It was contagious. I wanted to be in on the joke, so I decided to sit back and let it be, see what happens."

"And now, you're trying to carefully navigate dating one of your friends who happens to also be someone you work with, eh?"

Dad starts to bob his head up and down, and I can see from the expression on his face he's pleased I get it. Only when he looks over at me, he finds me sitting here in my chair, arms crossed with *that* look.

"Uh-uh." He wags a finger in the air. "I see what you just did there."

"Yeah, good. Now, you'll understand why I want everyone to lay off and leave me to it. Too many opinions around me, and let's face it, life is complicated enough right now."

Pushing my chair back, I stand up and gather my things. "I am a patient woman. You let me know when you're ready for me to meet her as your other half, and I'm there. I understand the feelings you're having. Out of sorts, insecure, the wondering...and the nerves."

"Yeah, you nailed it." Dad chuckles as he stands up and pulls his wallet out of his back pocket. "My turn this week."

As he makes his way over to the cashier's stand to pay for our brunch, I can't help but be in awe of him. My dad. My brave, amazing, strong, loving, perfectly imperfect father.

To think after all this time without someone in his life, he's found someone to hang with. A person who makes him happy and all lit up on the outside. As his daughter, I can't ask for anything more, can I?

Except to have my own happy ending with my best friend...but how am I going to get to that?

ELEVEN

Reid

In the time I've been on the roster at the station, Dubs's Garage has always been the place to go in town to get your car fixed. Well, it's actually one of two places, but if you're in the fire department, you had better go to Dubs or you were going to hear about it.

He'd gotten the garage for a steal, or so it's been said, and what he didn't have to pay for in the initial purchase of the station, he made sure to invest it into the renovation. He started by painting the outside bright yellow and orange, with reds to highlight, taking a cue from the look of old Shell stations from the sixties and seventies. The two gas pumps outside were both painted bright orange, too, and he'd gone to the trouble of having garden beds put in as well. Either he or Dylan had them set up with a rotation of seasonal flowers popping up every few months.

Inside, now that's where the fun begins. His garage is his workspace, but the lobby area has been made into the perfect room—the Man Cave as Dubs has labeled it—at least, it was until Dylan came along. Not one to have the label put off any other gender, she insists we call it The Cave now, if we're talking about it. And believe me. We do.

Dubs brought in some old-school pinball machines, which are so my thing. I used to own a few arcade games myself, but have since sold them to my brother-in-law, Ari's husband, Carter, when he opened his restaurant last year. We managed to wrangle one of them, PacMan, back and Dubs found a Ms. PacMan machine in mint condition that we added a few months ago. Someone donated an overstuffed couch, and I'd helped Dylan find a couple of recliners that we'd picked up together. I was touched at the time when she'd asked me to help pick them out, and I remember feeling warm and happy that I was the one she wanted to do that task with.

It also helps that Dubs is the best mechanic around. I've heard stories of him saving folks money or saving their cars more than once. And it's the place where I find myself on this sunny Monday morning getting an oil change before my shift starts.

I'm sitting on a chair in the lobby area, which is connected to the garage by a doorway. Dubs likes to keep it open so he can chit chat with customers hanging out and waiting for their cars. There's an office off to the side where Dylan sits with Max when she's here. It's a tiny spot with no natural light, but she'd managed to drag a couple of floor lamps in to add some ambiance, a chaise lounge for her dad to take naps on if he needed, plus Max's ginormous dog bed.

"Were you trying to run your truck into the ground this time?" Dubs asks, wiping off dark smudges of grease onto a giant towel as he strides into the lobby from the garage.

Before Dylan moved here, he was always wiping his hands on his coveralls. Let me tell you, those coveralls would get ripe. Between the man's lack of enjoyment for doing laundry and straight-up dude laziness, Dubs was pretty lucky his daughter moved here and started taking care of him. He was a bit of a grizzly bear back then.

I put the magazine down that I'd been rifling through for the last twenty minutes.

"It's on its last leg, Dubs. I'm taking care of it. I just think it's eating through the oil now." Or I, too, had some straight-up dude laziness in me that I'm just not willing to admit to at the moment. "Isn't the important thing that I got it here in time?"

Shaking his head, he ambles into the tiny office and motions for me to follow. Standing up, I'm about to take my first step when a familiar voice calls out from the street. By the time I turn around to see who it is, Dylan stands in front of me with one hand on her hip and a sexy smile draped across her mouth.

She eyes me while I fight the urge to stare at her rosy lips. "I thought we're working on the same shift today?"

Keep your eyes on hers, Reid. Keep it together, man. "We are, I just wanted to get my oil changed."

"Got it." She inclines her head toward the office. "I'm here to get my dog. He's got a playdate at the doggy day care today, but Dad stole him this morning."

I follow Dylan as she makes her way inside the office to find a very happy Max, looking like he just won the lottery sitting on Dubs's lap getting his paws rubbed.

Dylan groans and rolls her eyes. "You're kidding me. This is why he wants to come with you in the mornings? You bribing him with paw massages?"

"Well, if someone rubbed my feet every time I hung out with them, I bet I'd hang out with them more." His eyes find mine over Dylan's shoulder. "Am I right?"

Shaking my head, I chuckle. "I can't argue. A foot rub sounds amazing."

"You're both as bad as the other." Dylan leans over and

plucks a very zenned-out Max from his spot on Dubs's lap. "Amelia called and she's taking her dog to the daycare place in Sweetkiss for the first time, so I told her I'd meet her there before my shift. We're going to have Barney the beagle go in with Max the wonder mutt."

Dubs rolls his eyes. "You have got to be kidding me. Doggy daycare? Like dogs go to...daycare?"

Laughing, Dylan walks around her desk and opens a drawer, pulling out a small bag of what I know are Max's favorite doggy treats and his favorite leash, which is also her favorite, too. How do I know these things? Because I got them for her as a gift last year, a matching leash and collar set. No reason why, I just had seen them when I was out one day doing errands and knew Dylan would dig it.

Like the planner she clutches in her hands on a daily basis. People always tease her for having it all the time, and though I'm not into those things, I know it's a great planner. Mostly because I remember the day Dylan saw it when we walked past the local stationary shop.

We'd grabbed ice cream cones, and if I remember correctly, the ice cream was already melting because it was so warm on that November day, which is weird for North Carolina. We were racing to lick it off our hands when she stopped in her tracks and pointed at the display window. Her eyes were wide, and she explained how she loved that style of planner because of all it could do and how great it would be for organizing her life.

Did it seem nuts to me? You bet. But it's what she likes and she was telling me at that moment "here is this thing that I like. I want you to know more about me." At least that's how I took it, so the next day when we got to work I surprised her at the start of the shift with it. And she's carried it with her every day since.

"Yes, Dad, dogs go to daycare. Max had a healthy circle of

friends and a weekend playgroup when we lived in L.A." She cuts her eyes in my direction. "Max was very popular, you know."

Nodding, I lean against the doorway. There's a warmth spreading inside of me I can't explain, but this moment, this conversation and its ease with the ribbing and the jokes? It feels like home.

"I'm sure he was." Max is sitting on the floor in his matching collar and leash, grooming his long silver fur and sneaking me a serving of side-eye every few seconds. "He's a handsome devil. A silver fox, if you will."

Rubbing his beard, which is threaded with specks of silver as well, Dubs leans back on the small couch and grins much like I would imagine Santa would.

"Connie calls me her silver fox."

My jaw hits the floor.

"Connie?" I look at Dylan, whose face is bright red. It matches Dubs's, who won't make eye contact with me.

"Okay, then." Dylan slams the drawer shut and looks pointedly at her father, with a tiny grin playing on her lips. "We don't need to hear about your tawdry personal life. I'm outta here." She bends down and grabs Max's leash, turning to me as she breezes past. "Oh, by the way, I've got an idea for your date with Etta."

"My date with Etta?" My eyes bounce back and forth between Dylan and Dubs. "You mean, your date with Zac, right?"

"I said what I said." Right then, her cell phone dings, signaling a text. Dylan pulls her phone from her bag and looks at the screen before shoving it back into her purse. "I need to go. We can debate this further at work."

We both watch as Hurricane Dylan leaves the premises, navigating her way through the garage bay as she talks to Max and moves at the pace of a New Yorker on a mission.

Turning back around, I brush my hair out of my eyes and put Dubs in my sights.

"So. Connie?"

Dubs shakes his head. "First, let's discuss the crush you have on my daughter and the fact you've never done a thing about it."

Thankfully I have enough decorum to keep my jaw from smacking the concrete floor. Swallowing the lump in my throat, which is probably my pride, I slowly nod my head and look at the floor. Dubs is someone I've always had the utmost respect for. Since I started at the fire station, he's always been there for me with advice, career feedback, or to lend a hand. He's even shown up to help my family rebuild our house one year when the lake flooded and we had to redo the whole first floor, and he's helped both Ari and my mother when they ran out of gas one time on a back road in the middle of the night.

I have so much respect for this man—and he just called me out.

"Okay." My eyes stay glued to the floor. If he looks into them, I know he'll see my thoughts.

"Look at me, Reid." Dubs cackles, and without even looking up, I can tell from the soft patting sounds filling the room he's motioning for me to come sit and join him. "Come on. Sit here and let's talk for a sec."

My feet obey even though the rest of me is literally freaking out. I could lob the distraction ball here, shout out "what's up with Connie, old man?" and not only get him fired up about Connie but also about being called old, cause I know that gets him. But no. I trod over slowly and lower myself beside him, sitting just on the edge hoping I'm out of reach if he suddenly decides he wants to reach out and slap me.

"I'm only going to say this to you once, because I am not the kind of parent who wants to ever get involved in their kids' love life, but I need to say this now." He leans back into the comfort of the couch cushions, angling his body toward mine. It's a move that naturally puts me at ease but just enough that I can sit back, stiffly, against the cushions myself. I keep my body angled to jump up fast if I need to, though.

"Look, Reid, what are you two doing?" He shakes his head and tilts it to one side, watching me. "When Dylan moved here, I was worried she wouldn't find it appealing. She'd hate it. I knew she was coming for me, and boy, was there pressure. I didn't want to be the reason she was unhappy if she didn't like it here."

"I remember that. You asked me and some of the other guys to make sure we hung out with her." I do remember it, like it happened only yesterday. We were all the probies—the newer officers on probation at the station while we proved ourselves. "All of us were a little wary of how she'd slot in and if she'd be cool hanging out with us, then she rolled up on the first day and kicked our butts playing pool one night. Hustler."

"She walked away that first night raving about everyone. Especially the goofy blond guy who kept everyone laughing."

Turning my head, I look at Dubs, whose eyes twinkle in the low light. "You took her under your wing that night and I've always been appreciative, but I see what's happened. The relationship that's blossomed now, and I have to know, Reid —what are you going to do about it?"

Now I let my jaw hit the floor. This man has my number.

"Honestly, Dubs, I'm not sure what to do about it." Steeling myself, I think about my words carefully. "She seems intent that I need to go on a date with Etta, she's been kind of lobbying for it, and somehow we're all going out on a group date now." I shake my head and look at my friend, hoping he can see the plea for advice in my expression. Holding my hands up in surrender, I stand up. "I feel like I've been backed into a no-win situation at the moment."

"Talk to me."

Sighing, I clasp my hands together and stare at the ground so I can say what I need to. "I want to—I've been wanting to ask Dylan to go out on a date with me for a long time." Man, it feels so good to say it. The knot in my stomach begins to unravel, so I take another breath and continue. "Your daughter makes me mental and also brings me the greatest joy on any given day of the week. The fact she's even contemplating leaving the area and going back to L.A. strikes fear inside of me, because I do not know what I would do without her in my life."

"She's what?" Dubs sits up straight, his eyes wide and our moment of bonding now thrust aside. "When did she say that?"

Seeing the look on Dubs's face, I'm pretty sure I just opened my fat mouth where I wasn't supposed to. "No, it's nothing set in stone. She was just throwing out ideas when she realized you guys needed to sell the house."

His words of wisdom have quickly fallen to the wayside as a wave of emotions washes over his face. "If she moves back to the other side of the country because of me, I won't be able to stand it, Reid."

"I know. And I'm going to do everything in my power to keep her here, too." Nodding, I step forward and pat him on his shoulder. "I mean it, Dubs."

A few moments later, I'd paid for my oil change and pulled out of the garage, and watched Dubs walk away with his head hung low, matching my own mood. Knowing what they're going through, I wish I had a magic wand I could wave and make it all go away. I want to help.

And that big talk about keeping her here? Now I have to make it happen.

It's time to put on my big boy pants and get the girl.

TWELVE

Dylan

Moving around the tiny home I share with my dad, I grab some tape and flattened cardboard boxes from a pile stacked on the dining room table. I need to keep my hands as busy as I can so my mind stays busy, too. Taping up the cardboard boxes Dad purchased from U-Haul over the weekend is filling the need.

I'd decided to cast a line out, feelers if you will, and see if my old job and moving back to California was something in the cards for me, and after a quick catchup over Zoom, I can officially say that the part of my life that was there can be put to bed.

I was nervous when the call started, but as soon as I saw my old colleagues from A List Events, the feeling evaporated as fast as it had come on. My tummy did a little dance of happiness seeing my old friends, who I've missed. Seeing their smiling faces sitting at the conference table—albeit on the other side of the country—was like Christmas. I even got a gift out of it, too—the gift of self-realization, when it sinks in that you've moved on from something and it's time to say goodbye.

Soft tapping on the front door grabs my attention. I pause for a second, thinking I'm hearing things when the taps come again. This time, more firmly than before.

Frowning, I cast my eyes around the room at the mess I'm in the middle of, cringing at the upheaval, and look at my watch. Dad's still on his shift and I'm not expecting anyone.

"Hey, Dylan." More knocking. "I know you're there. Dubs said you were here packing."

Hearing his voice through the door, my heart skips an actual for real beat in my chest. How is it that someone can be this one kind of person in your world for years, this someone who is the kind of friend you can ask if you have food in your teeth or the person who gets your little jokes and ticks, maybe even knows your favorite candy bar? (For the record, Reid's is Snickers, because it's as good as a meal in his book.) Then, one day, things change and you feel different. Like there's a balloon inside of your heart and it needs to escape before it pops, but it's so wonderful and heady, like a rush of adrenaline when you get too close to the edge of a steep cliff, and you almost want to stay suspended. Stock still, right here in this state of knowing and yet not knowing, for as long as you can because if you break the trance you're in....

Then it's all over.

"Dylan!" More knocking, but there's a change in his tactic. Reid's singing. "I've got lunch for you."

Laughing, I unlock the door, shaking off my ridiculous inner monologue at the same time. It's me. It's Reid. It's us.

Throwing open the door, I'm not prepared for shirtless Reid who fills my doorway, staring down at me with that insanely lazy but sexy "I know something that you don't" smile on his lips. He holds up a brown paper bag in both hands, and it's falling apart.

"I stopped and got you some pad thai, but"—he looks

over his shoulder, where the T-shirt he must have had on previously is slung—"I managed to spill my Thai iced tea down the front of myself when I hit the brakes for Little Timmy."

"Seriously? That kid is a stinking menace." I step out of his way and hold out my hand, ushering him in. "Did he run out in front of your truck?"

Reid nods. "It's like he wanted to play chicken with my truck's grill."

"Good timing, I was about to make something." Locking the door behind me, I mentally prepare myself for what I'm about to see. It's one thing to see Reid changing at work, because we're at work in go-mode, but with the way my head has been lately and now having him here, in front of me, shirtless...I swallow and swallow hard, preparing myself.

Who am I kidding? There is no preparation for moments like this. I turn around and find him standing there, the waist of his jeans clinging to that part of his body where there's a nice perfect V, the definition all but popping on his glistening skin. I let my eyes make their way upward, dragging them slowly along his toned midsection. I'm on the Reid Highway of Hotness, making the climb up to the Summit of Swoon when he clears his throat, snapping me out of my fog.

"I was in the neighborhood. I'm on call today, so I can't stay long but thought I could swing by and help you eat while you work," he teases.

Busted, I pretend he's not shirtless and smack his arm playfully. "Watch out for the boxes, and apologies in advance if you get any shots of my underwear or other feminine delicates. Dubs messed up my box system when I was on shift with you yesterday, and I'm still trying to figure out where Max's winter jackets are."

Reid plonks the bag on the coffee table before scooping up

a very happy Max into his arms, kissing his little head. I'll never get over how adorable it is to see a man like Reid, all muscle and tanned skin—looking insanely hot and handsome as well—holding a small dog and giving it cuddles.

WITH HIS SHIRT OFF.

"The fact Max has several winter jackets tells me there's an issue here." Cradling Max, he turns to face me, Max's tongue rolling out of his mouth in pure joy as he receives tummy scratches.

I feel you buddy. Trust.

"The issue being I even have jackets for my dog?" I get it. I've heard enough about my dog's fashion since moving here. "Back in L.A, Max was fashion, honey," I say with a little French accent, stepping closer to the cute duo so I can scratch Max between his ears. "Now that we're in the sticks, he needs to be even more over-the-top."

"Very *Schitt's Creek* of him."

"Pretty much." Spotting a box that has some of my dad's cast-offs in it, I peel open the lid and dig inside. I'm rewarded, finding an old T-shirt that I pull up and toss over to Reid. "Here. Cover up, would ya?"

He steps in toward me so we're standing really close together. So close that Reid's scent is on the tip of my tongue and I can smell his soap through the layers of other smells he has. I know, it's ridiculous, but I can tell the smell of his laundry detergent versus the scent I get from his shampoo and conditioner. I have a nose like a wolf.

I also know there are days he uses his favorite cologne, which is the sandalwood scent I adore so much, but he also has one that's a cleaner smell, like fresh sheets, which I believe is his aftershave.

Yeah, Reid, I have issues. They have nothing to do with Max.

Thankfully, Reid pulls the T-shirt over his head and sadly moves his chest away from me, but it's good. I need a moment to calm down the kitten in heat that's taken over my body all of a sudden. We both scratch a very lucky Max, Reid massaging his paws as he cradles him in his arms while I tickle his tummy lightly with the tips of my fingers. If I'm not mistaken, it seems that Reid's fingers are starting to gain some ground on Max as they invade his tummy area, too.

Slowly, I drag my eyes up to meet Reid's. He stares at me, watching me, his lips turned up at the corners and his eyes gleaming. I'm taken off guard, my fingers touching his as they intertwine in a chance encounter on sweet Max's little pink stomach.

My breath hitches, and I know it's a cheesy alignment, but it feels like I'm caught in the tractor beam from Star Wars. I cannot look away from this man. I see safety and love, laughter and light, there's comfort and peace and it's all wrapped up inside of him.

Reid dips his chin, eyes narrowing as they fall to my lips. Normally, I'd make a joke about him looking at me like this, break the moment, and get back to being goofy us.

But I don't want that right now. I allow my eyes to make their way down to savor his lips, licking my own slowly as I do. Have I thought about kissing Reid? Every day for months.

Still holding Max, Reid leans over and taps his forehead to mine and the energy around us is forever changed, heightened and sparking in that one second.

"Hi." His voice is a raspy whisper.

"Hi." Pressing my lips together, I smile. Our foreheads still touch, and I can't move. How did a surprise lunch delivery tip over into this moment and so fast? My heart races and my mind moves a million miles a minute—did I brush my teeth? Am I sure I want to kiss him now? Should we put Max down?

I pull away slightly, but Reid's angled himself so he's even closer, therefore his lips are too. Everything inside me both stalls and quickens, all at once. My palms are clammy and my mouth is surprisingly dry, but there's a tingle racing through my body. Slowly and purposefully, I reach out and take Max from his grasp and bend over to gently place him on the floor beside us. As I stand back up, Reid's hand takes me by the elbow, his eyes boring a hole deep into mine, studying me and holding me. His touch feels like a flame licking my arm.

Reaching his hand up toward my face, he pushes some stray strands of hair out of my eyes. "I came over here with the intention of telling you something today."

Closing my eyes, I let the moment settle over me. His one hand on my arm, and now his other hand wrapping its way around my waist, pulling me into him. As my body leans against his, in my mind I'm taken back to the dance floor at Maisey and Jack's wedding and the very same thrill that had rushed through me that day is back.

Lost in his spell, my hands thread their way around his neck. "I'm happy you showed up with food."

Tossing his head back, he laughs before dipping his chin so we're back on eye level again, and his breath hits my cheek. "I've known you a long time, Dylan, and I'd be a liar if I tried to act like I didn't have some kind of feelings for you by now."

Swallowing the lump in my throat, all I can do is slowly nod my head in agreement. I keep my eyes on him, letting the gravelly tone of his voice shred my insides to pieces.

"You're my best friend, you know that?"

My breath hitches as his grip tightens around my waist, pulling me closer to him, his body firm as he holds me against it. I've waited for this for so long, I want to enjoy every little step we take.

I allow my fingers to trace a trail down the side of his face, skimming along his jawline, his eyes closing as I do, a sigh escaping from his lips.

"I do," I whisper back, unsure where to go next.

And while I may be unsure, Reid isn't. His thumb tips my chin as he pulls me in closer, our noses touching and softly nuzzling, my skin grazing across his with the soft heat of our combined friction making me tremble.

What are we doing?

Right before Reid arrived, I was considering going back to California. I'm packing up my home because my poor dad is up to his ears in debt and we need to fix things. I want to fix things for him, and that makes my life way more complicated at this moment than it needs to be.

As Reid skims my lips with his thumb, my mind races. It feels so good and oh-so-right, but what do I have to offer him? He's an amazing guy, and I'm someone who needs to focus on immediate family matters. I can't be in this mode right now, even though I want to be.

And then there's Etta. What kind of woman am I to act like I'm trying to set someone up on a date, then I go off and make out with him? Not that we've made out yet, but we're headed there—this is definitely making-out territory and we're deep in it. Close to the edge, on the precipice, here it comes if I'm not careful...

But I want to. That's the worst part. Or maybe it's the best?

As Reid tilts his head and leans in, closing the last tiny thread of the space between us, the tinkling sounds of steel drum wonderment in a Caribbean calypso band goes off from my back pocket.

Gripping me tighter, Reid presses his forehead into mine again, shaking his head. "Don't answer it."

The grit in his voice is like catnip, and I want to nibble on it, but the sound still chimes around us.

For me, this sound is like being pulled out of a hypnotic state, which I am grateful for right now. Am I feeling major sparks and a physical pull that I'm not in any way, shape, or form ready to deal with right now? Yes, I am. And it's not that I'm not ready to deal with it, I just don't have time right now.

Who am I kidding? I don't want to be hurt. And I don't want to be the one who hurts someone. Especially Reid.

His breath hits my cheek as the Calypso band starts another round, so I do the unthinkable.

Stepping away, I break our bubble of heat and indecision and pull the phone from my pocket. Seeing Etta's name on the screen, I take it as a sign from the universe and hit the answer icon, pressing the phone to my ear.

"Hey, Etta, what's up?"

Reid crosses his arms in front of his chest, his cheeks flushed as red as the fire engines we ride on as he watches me talk to Etta. I'm hazy, listening to her quandary, and my guilt has me agreeing to meet her to look at a space she wants to rent out at Amelia and Spencer's campground. We make a date for an hour from now, and I disconnect, sitting down on the couch to catch my breath.

A few quiet moments later, Reid sits down beside me. "Dylan, what are we doing?"

Leaning forward, I open the bag of food and start pulling out take-out boxes. "We're going to have our lunch like two grown adults who are friends, that's what we're doing."

"That's the thing, Dylan." Reid stands, pushing his hair back with his right hand as he paces the living room floor in front of me. "We're friends. Best friends, but I've been having a lot of introspective moments here lately and…"

The sound of a pager beeping at an alarming pitch breaks the conversation up. Reid's hand flies to his hip as he pulls the pager off. "Oh man, I gotta go."

He heads to the front door, turning to face me as he

throws it open. "We're not done yet, Dylan." He looks at me pointedly. "I mean it. We're not done here yet."

With that, he slams the door shut behind him and races to the fire station, leaving me breathless in the middle of my living room with my pad thai, a worked-up nervous system, and some thinking to do.

THIRTEEN

Dylan

Pulling into the campground parking lot, I'm instantly impressed with the layout. On my drive across the country to move from California to North Carolina, I'd seen many campgrounds advertised as I flew past them. Growing up with Dubs, you bet we spent a few summers out camping, so I saw campgrounds up and down the west coast in those days, too.

I guess that could make me somewhat of a campground connoisseur. "Loves a firm mattress, but will take the top bunk if needed" was me in my day. But when we camped in our tents, I loved the whole "let's get dirty and relax" vibe it gave us. Freedom to do whatever we wanted whenever we wanted to.

Opening my car door, I jump out. Etta stands with Amelia at one end of the parking lot, looking out over an expanse of field. Waving, I push my guilt way to the back of my head and out of my mind. So I almost kissed the guy I'm trying to set Etta up with, but it's not like it happened, so we're fine. I'm fine.

I walk a little faster to make my way over to them, glancing at my watch to make sure I'm not running late.

"I beat you here." Etta's ear-to-ear smile looks painted on perfect. She spins around in a circle and holds her arms out wide. "Isn't this gorgeous? This is why I moved to the south, to get fresh air and wide spaces like this."

Beside her, Amelia laughs, pulling me into a hug. "I love it when people get excited about the little things. Reminds us we're alive."

"I'm just excited. All the time these days, but that's how I run. Buzzing at a high level of energy, pretty much." Etta steps around Amelia to embrace me as well. I guess we do that now? So I'm okay with hugging the woman I want to set up with the man I'm in love with?

Yep. All good.

Amelia looks behind me, as if something is missing. "No Reid today?"

Shaking my head, my eyes bounce back and forth between the two women, who both smile at me. "Should I have brought him?"

Amelia shakes her head, placing one hand squarely on her hip. "I figured he'd be with you. It's like a peanut butter sandwich not having jelly, or Kool Aid without sugar."

Unsure where this is going or why it's come up, I fidget. Changing the subject, I point to the large space behind them. "Is this field for camping overflow?"

Amelia nods, pointing to the other side of the field where the forest begins. "Lorelei Woods starts there, and we have several areas cleared out inside of the trees for RVs and campers, both to set up their sites. But the field is here in case we fill those spaces up, plus we're going to use it for event rentals." Amelia crosses her arms and turns to me. "We're in talks to host the First Annual Sweetkiss Creek Dogwood

Festival here next year but, more importantly, we'll have the Sweetkiss Summer Series here this year!"

"That's great!" I clap my hands together before sheepishly looking at Amelia and Etta, who both look at me like I'm one brick shy of a load. "No, really, it is. Lake Lorelei used to host it, but the town square is too small now for how many people show up. It's so much fun!"

Amelia motions for us to follow her, so we both fall in line beside her and walk back to the main buildings.

"What is it all about? Spencer is the one who okayed it, not me." I detect irritation in Amelia's voice, but since we've only just graduated from two people who have dogs and maybe-we-have-something-in-common to hugging when we say hello, I'm not going to push it.

"For three months, the Summer Series committee works to put on events that will bring out locals and bring in tourists all summer long. They organize movie nights, festivals and fairs, antique car shows—you name it. If it's outside, during summer, and can attract a crowd, they give it a go."

Amelia slows her pace down on our approach to the first of three single-story buildings. Each building resembles a squatter version of the traditional log cabin, with each boasting two entrances off of the porch, leading into separate retail spaces.

"Here's the spot I think could work for you." Pulling a key out, she marches up the steps of one of the cabins, unlocking the door. "It needs some TLC; the folks who owned this place before us were older. They'd let it go for the last few years, so we have some renovating to do, but this is the best of the bunch."

As the door swings open, I watch as Etta's mouth does, too.

"Let it go" is an understatement.

"Oh, boy." She steps inside the doorway ahead of us, her

head turning from side to side as she looks around. "I mean, it's got good bones?'

I'm hot on her heels, crossing the threshold behind her, and I see what she means. It's a bit of dumpster fire, that's for sure. Old moldy boxes sit piled in erratic positions in one corner of the room, and I'm pretty sure that's a rat's nest in the other corner...and I think it just moved.

I want to find the right words, because I don't want her to be disappointed. Plus I need to appease my own guilt. "It's got...potential?"

Amelia snorts. "You two are so full of Southern belle syndrome. It's horrible!"

All three of us burst into laughter. Etta wipes tears from her cheeks—from laughter, worry, or allergies, I'm not sure.

"So, obviously there is a lot of work that needs to happen to this place to get it going, but the reason I wanted you to see this particular one was because of what's in the back. Follow me." Amelia steps over a pile of old newspapers, and I fight the urge to point and yell "fire hazard," and leads us to a room beyond the one we're in.

As Etta walks through the doorway ahead of me, I hear the sigh of happiness as it escapes from her lips.

"Ohhh, yes. What is that doing here?"

On one side of the wall is a giant, built-in refrigerator unit with glass doors. Amelia steps forward and flicks on a switch, illuminating the insanely filthy case for us to see it and its contents. I'm pretty sure the owner of the rat's nest in the front room just scurried past, but never mind.

Amelia grins at Etta's reaction. "The last person who rented this was a florist, and they had a special bespoke case made for the space so they could make use of it."

Clicking my tongue on the roof of my mouth, I realize I need to be the bearer of bad news. "But it's a floral fridge. A wine fridge needs different temperature controls inside for beverages, especially wine." Turning to Etta, I shrug a shoulder. "You did ask me to come along to give my opinion. Plus you need to be careful with humidity levels, right?"

Slowly Etta nods her head in agreement, looking over at Amelia. "She's right. It's a great unit—"

"And it can be refurbished with the controls you need for a wine cooler." Amelia announces the last sentence with excitement and thrill as she hands Etta a card. "I spoke to a local electrician who said he could do the refurbish. We just need to get him in to do a quote."

Etta stands with her hands crossed in front of her chest, surveying the space and the business card. The look on her face and the way she has her mouth twisted reminds me of Reid, a tiny thing to notice but something that makes my tummy dip when I think about it, nonetheless.

Amelia must sense the same hesitancy I do coming off Etta's pores. She steps forward and places a hand on her arm. "You can always go away and think about it, let me know later this week if it's a project you're into attacking."

Etta squats down, into the perfect prayer position for yoga, still entranced and looking around.

Nudging my arm, Amelia leans in closer to me. "She okay?"

"Appears that way." I nod my head slowly. "I think she's taking it all in."

She watches Etta, quirking her head to one side. "It's a lot of mess to handle."

Glancing around at the cobwebs on the ceiling, I shudder. "You're telling me."

A moment later, Etta hops up from her squatting position and does this funny little thing where she jogs in place while taking a few deep breaths. Reminding me again of someone we both know.

"You're starting to take on Reid-isms." I manage to get it

out with a hint of a laugh at the end of my words. But she does remind me of him right now. Which also means I'm thinking of him, and I need to get those thoughts of him out of my mind. Especially when I'm pretty sure Etta would be a good fit for Reid.

All I can think about now is how he almost kissed me earlier. Touching his face, his soft skin, and breath saturated with the scent of peppermint and cupcakes, which is surprising because it's Reid. I wish I would have just leaned in and let his soft lips...

"Guess I'm hanging at the fire station too much these days." Etta says it with a chuckle as she faces Amelia, thus snapping me out of my daydream like a whip had cracked the air. "Okay, so what's the deal again?'

"We're open to whatever you think about this space, honestly." We follow Amelia outside to the porch, watching as she locks the doors. "To be honest, we weren't prepared to invest in all of these cabins right now since we dumped all of our money into the campground and the art gallery. But when I met you and heard your predicament...I don't know. It seems like this was meant to be and I'd love to find a way to get you into this space. It just has to work for both of us."

"I'll go and crunch some numbers, come up with a plan, and let's meet up again in a few days?" I can hear the hope in Etta's voice. Looking at the cabin, there's no doubt it would be a great place to set up a tasting room, but the amount of work that needs to go into it first is going to take a strong woman to lead it. Which is indeed Etta.

"Sounds good." Amelia looks at her watch and her eyes grow wide. "Yikes, I'm late for our other cabin inspection."

Looking at the small buildings around us, I look back to Amelia. "One of these?"

"No, it's tucked back in the woods. If you look on the other side of the field, you'll see it right at the tree line."

Following her finger and where she points, I spy the tiny log cabin she's talking about. Similar in style to the buildings we're in front of, it has two floors and is surrounded by a small fence, setting it apart from all the other spots here on the campground.

"That is going to be where our campground manager will live." Amelia smiles. "Luckily, that house is in great shape. We're going to have it cleaned this week so it's ready when we start looking at applications for the job in a few weeks' time."

My mouth falls open, incredulous. "That's part of the hire package?"

Beside me, Etta lets out a low whistle. "Sweet."

Amelia spins on her heel and sets Etta in her sights. "It's not something you'd want to do, is it?"

"Manage a campground?" Etta's brow furrows as she mulls it over. "I probably could, but I don't think I have the energy nor the basic knowledge to be of help." She looks at me sheepishly. "I've never been camping."

"You don't need to know camping to do it; you'd be managing the grounds and being my eyes and ears here. And from the sounds of things, taking on event organization with the summer series and the dogwood festival." Amelia looks at me. "What about you?"

What about me? I have no clue how to answer this right now. Do I think I could run a campground when I'm not on an ambulance shift? I do have experience with events, but is this where I see myself in the future?

Then there's Reid. And Etta. And our double date coming up that I'm sure will cement for both of them that they'd be good together. And the moment I had with Reid earlier today? Weak moment. Two friends who got their wires crossed for a second. It can happen. I know it can, even though I cannot for the life of me think of any examples of this right now.

But I could also go back to L.A., even though it's like a shoe that doesn't fit any more. Slip back into my old job working events and coordinating the most epic parties ever. Back to days of high heels and timelines and deadlines, and the rush of the 101 highway. They offered me more money per week to come back than I make working on the ambulance in a month.

But it's L.A. and it is just...different. You can't ever go home again, and I'm ready for that chapter to close. There's no Dubs, no quiet streets. No Riley, no knowing the majority of the folks you see when you walk down the street. And there's no Reid.

However, there's been a lot of change around here lately. The obvious issues at home go unstated, Dad is dating, Reid has a roommate. I have to find a place to live....WOW. My internal monologue needs to shut up. I'm worn out.

"Hello?" Amelia shakes my arm gently. "You still with us?"

"Sorry." Shaking my head, I plaster a smile across my face. Even showing my teeth. "I forgot that I'm supposed to be home helping Dad with his...inventory. Slipped my mind until a few moments ago."

Sue me, so I'm fibbing. But my mind is racing and I want to be alone in my car, stat.

"You know, I need to get going as well." Etta, who had plopped herself on the porch steps, hops up, grabbing her purse as she does. She smiles at Amelia. "Thank you for your time today. I'll be in touch."

Waving, Amelia jogs away in the direction of the tiny log cabin before we both turn around and make the walk across the gravel parking lot to our cars. Pulling my keys from my bag, I wave to Etta as I press on the key fob to remotely unlock my doors, and then I open the driver's side.

"Thanks again for coming today, I really appreciate it."

She grins and taps the roof of her car as she leans against it. "I've got some thinking to do, that's for sure."

"I'm glad I could help." Help with what, though? Determined to clear my head and quiet my mind, I throw myself inside the safety of my car to be alone with my crazy thoughts.

FOURTEEN

Reid

When I was in high school, and my sister was on the school newspaper, I remember her making a big deal every time she typed "the end" on one of her stories, big or small. I would tease her, asking her why she needed the attention and the applause after getting something done that I saw, at the time, as ridiculously easy.

Then, during my senior year of high school, I had to write my first article. I was the captain of the football team and we were headed to the state championship. Our coaches wanted one of the players to write about the year we'd had, but they wanted it to be a feature article on the whole team, with the object to get our town rallied behind us before the big game. Since I was captain and the great junior journalist Ari Shannon's brother, of course they thought I was the best one for the job. Begrudgingly, I said yes.

I think I was on my fifteenth draft and about to call my coach and beg to have someone else do the work, when Ari came into my room to borrow something. She must have seen the crumpled sheets of paper all over my floor, the haphazard way my desk was organized, and books from *How to write a newspaper article* to *Elements of Style* strewn everywhere. I'm pretty sure I looked crazy, too. There may or may not have been a shower that day.

My sister sat with me that Saturday afternoon, when she could have been out anywhere else with anyone else doing anything else, and helped me to work on that article. She wouldn't write it for me—believe me, I asked. I offered her cash. She still said no, but she did stay by my side and answer questions I had about style, then agreed to edit it for me after I was done.

That day, when I typed "the end" on my first newspaper write-up—that took way too many man hours to organize—I understood why she always marked the occasion. I took us out for ice cream to celebrate.

Now, here I am. Just a man, standing in front of the freezer, looking for his pint of rocky road so he can mark the occasion. That's right, I typed "the end." Well, Andrew did, but I'm going to make sure I celebrate for him, because I have it on good account he'd want to.

After moving the bags of frozen vegetables around that Zac managed to stockpile into our tiny freezer, I still cannot find what I'm after. I give up. If I didn't eat it and it's gone, there's only one way it would have left the building.

I make my way to the back of the house, pausing to rap on Zac's closed bedroom door. "Yo, you here, Zac?"

"Enter!"

Putting my hand on the door handle, I open the door and poke my head inside. What greets me is not what I expected.

At all.

"Hey, man." Zac looks up at me from where he sits on the floor. "What's up?"

Coldplay is on in the background, and they're still yellow, while I'm here fighting shock. My face reacts before I have time to send it a signal to be cool, but luckily Zac's a pretty good guy, so when he sees my expression, he laughs and points at the material surrounding him.

"Guess you've never walked in on a grown man quilting before, have you?"

"I can't say that I have." Inspecting the piles on his bed, I grab at one and pluck a hunk of fabric out. "Is this an old Lake Lorelei Fire Department tee?"

Zak nods. "I heard one of the guys might be retiring this year, so I thought it was a good project to have on the side. You know, in case. If he does, we'll have a cool gift to give him, and if he doesn't, I'll gift it to the station anyway."

The man and the activity are just not syncing. I look at Zac, all six feet of him, strong build, dark hair, and sitting on the floor surrounded by sewing supplies. I can only shake my head. "I'm so confused."

"When I got stressed during police academy training, my nanny used to make me help her when I was home for the weekend. My stress had started to come out as pure anxiety, so she introduced me to quilting." Zac chuckles as he grabs a T-shirt from the pile and starts cutting it. "It really calms me down, and I can also make quilts really fast. Like lightning. If there was a contest, I'd enter it and win."

"You can always put some of this in the county fair." Holding up a few pieces of fabric he's sectioned together, I can actually see the delicate handiwork he's added to it, all defined in the stitching. "Though you'd be competing against little old ladies, would it make you happy to win?"

"One hundred percent. They're vicious. I hung out with my gran's sewing circle...you didn't mess with them." He grabs a pair of scissors and slices away some thread, rolling his eyes. "Especially Dorothy. If you didn't do your stippling stitch correctly, oh would you hear about it."

"Full of surprises." Tossing his handiwork back into the pile, I return to my original reason for bothering him. "I'm trying to find some ice cream that used to be in the freezer... know anything?"

"Yeah, man, sorry. I moved it to the deep freeze in your garage when I took over the kitchen freezer with my vegetables." He peers at me with a grin twisting on his lips. "You were prepared to come in here and flip out because you thought I ate it, didn't you?"

I take a play swipe at him before stepping back into the hall. "So what if I did? I'm a human in need of sugar."

"You sound like my sister."

"Yeah? Well, enjoy quilting." Before I close the door behind me, I hear Zac say something I can't make out, so I open the door back up. "What did you say?"

"I was just asking if you're sure Dylan's single?"

This is coming from left field, yet also not. Crossing my arms in front of my chest, I lean on the inside of the bedroom doorjamb.

"She is, but she's not your typical woman. Like, for dating."

Zac's brow furrows. "She's not my typical woman for dating, or she's not *the* typical woman who dates?"

A little of both? "Why are you asking?"

"I feel like I know someone's vibe, and the other night at the gallery I wasn't getting a vibe, you know?"

This is good. I'm beginning to think Zac may be second guessing pursuing a date with Dylan.

"Yeah." Shrugging, I let my tone come off as nonchalant. Let this play out, I remind myself. "Well, it could be she hasn't gone on a date in a long time. Maybe sitting down at dinner is a bit too much?"

"I thought of that, too!" Zac grabs his phone and shows me the latest write-up from Andrew Jenkins. My head almost spins off its axis. "A new escape room opened up in Sweetkiss Creek. This review in Culture Shock makes it sound awesome.

I was thinking instead of going out for a boring meal, let's all do that on our double date."

So now we're all calling it a double date? "I feel like 'group outing' is a more appropriate term here?"

"Whatever, man." Zac grins and settles with his back against the bed, picking up his quilting work again. But his grin dips for a second. "I wanted to ask, are you sure you aren't into her? Dylan?"

I have my chance. It's here. I can tell Zac now to back off, that yes, I have feelings for her. Granted, I've not told her about them yet, but I have them.

But am I a chicken who isn't opening his mouth right now? Why, yes. *Bawk bawk.*

However, I am a chicken who is grateful when his cell phone rings. Whipping it from my back pocket, I show the flashing screen to Zac. Mouthing the words "talk later," I back out of the room.

"I'm glad you called." It's Ari, so I take a second to update her on Andrew's work and she's thrilled. I can tell by the "woo hoo!!" that rings out in my ear as I make my way out to the deep freezer in the garage.

"You are the best, and you're in before the deadline! I adore you, Andrew, I mean Reid, I mean...who are you, anyway?"

I quickly open the freezer door, bend over and grab my prize, then close the door and head back inside. "I'm a man who's about to have some rocky road, that's who I am."

"Good man. One must always mark the occasion." Ari giggles in my ear, reinforcing my drive for sugar. "So, you're going to love this. Andrew is really becoming popular. In fact, I have some ridiculous news for you. We've had more requests for him to come try out more new businesses, but we also have old businesses in the area who are wondering if Andrew would be interested in coming to try them out, too?"

"I'm happy to do it, if you want me to keep going?"

"Oh my goodness, yes! Your column is the one that gets the most hits every time we load it. It's being shared everywhere."

My chest automatically swells with pride. Having high praise like this from my sister is kind of a big deal and I can't wait to tell Dylan...well, when she finally knows about Andrew, that is. She's going to crack up when I tell her about Zac and his quilting, too, but I digress.

My thoughts slide over to Dylan. It's like there's been a tiny glitch in my own internal matrix and just by simply thinking her name all I can see is her face, bright and happy, in front of me. And her lips. Those lips I almost kissed the other day. Beautiful, full, smooth, pink pillows...

"Reid?" The giant sigh slamming against my ear tells me I missed hearing something very important. "You're not even excited about this, are you?"

I wish I had heard it, that's what I think. "I'm so excited... no, I didn't hear you. Sorry."

Huffing, Ari starts over. "I offer to give you this gig as a permanent position on the paper, plus tell you we have found a publisher who is interested in backing a book, BY YOU, and you aren't even listening?" I can hear her eyes rolling back in her head. "What is wrong with you?"

"I'm...distracted." And now I'm floored. "Of course, that is...wow."

Yeah. Wow. The offer to keep doing the column? And a book? I take a moment for it to settle in. When it does, I have questions.

"You sure you've called the right number?" I tap on my phone for effect. "Hello? This is Reid Shannon, you know."

"You're ridiculous." Ari's voice changes, which means she's getting serious. "Look, Lake Lorelei and Sweetkiss Creek are bringing a lot of attention to Love Valley. Someone from

North Carolina tourism called our offices after reading your work. They love the voice, the fact it's such a smooth line between local and journalist. These people are raving about you, and their offices and executive team love you. They're the ones who want to offer to back a book with all of your columns featured. And any subsequent ones you do that we think would fit as well."

"Then what will the books be used for? Coasters? Bricks?"

"No, it's going to go into bookstores, Reid. For-real stores where people buy books. Online, too. I think someone mentioned audiobook rights, but that will all be laid out in the contract. We need to get an agent for you and fast because, honey, you just hit the big time!"

My head spins. In giant circles. Hula hoop circles. "Is there going to be a book launch with people there?"

"We didn't get that far, but I'm sure there will be. In fact, I'm happy to throw you one when the time comes if I have to." I can feel her giddy enthusiasm across the line. "It's up to you, but I think you—well, we since you did write the articles for *my* paper—should do it."

"What do you mean?"

"Well, Dad always asks if you're going to do anything with your life, and you *are*. In fact, with what you've written so far, you know you could get a job writing for another newspaper, a magazine, an art industry specific paper...not many journalists or columnists end up with a book offer in their first year of writing, but you have. I'd be over-the-top jealous about this if I wasn't so happy for you."

Now back in the kitchen, I take a bite of my rocky road ice cream right from the carton...actually I inhale another two spoonfuls because this guy? He's okay with eating his feelings. Although I'll need to add an extra mile to tomorrow's treadmill session, but that's okay.

She's right. She's more than right. This is something I

want to do. "I can't say no to this, Ari. It's a once in a lifetime thing and I want it."

"Are you sure?" Her voice has gone up an octave.

"Let's make it happen."

She squeals happily and with much enthusiasm in my ear, forcing me to pull the phone away for a second to right myself. I swear the pitch she hit threw me off balance. "Should I tell Mom and Dad, or do you want to?"

When I think about who I want to tell, only one person comes to mind. Of course, I want to share this with my parents, but it's Dylan who I want to finally let in on my secret. She's a fan of Andrew's; she'll get it.

I've been scared to tell anyone about my writing, really. Fear isn't a word I should use, though...more like self-doubt. Insecurity. Trying something out that no one expects of you and having them tell you that you suck at it. It's why I agreed to be anonymous, so I could feel the freedom of no judgment.

But now...a book deal? I'm the flipping Ernest Hemingway of Love Valley, thank you very much!

"Let's wait to tell Mom and Dad. I may sound superstitious, but I want to make sure the ink is dry on anything we sign before we share it." Not that they'd judge me, but I want time to digest this first, then explain to them how I've been working my butt off to gain traction in the world. Let them know they did right with how they raised me.

"Okay, I can respect that. Let me know when you finally want to tell them, though. I really want to be there to see their faces. They are going to flip."

"Speaking of flipping..." I can't hold it in any longer. I unleash the events at Dylan's on my little sister. Who, thankfully, reacts as strongly as I need her to right now.

"What? I would have thought you had that in the bag, Reid! What happened?"

"I wish I knew. We were fine, in fact it was like...it was on par with one of those movies you like watching so much."

"A romance? Or are we talking rom-com?"

"While our day-to-day is definitely rom-com, this was romance." My heart skips an extra beat at the thought. "I wanted to kiss her and could tell she wanted to kiss me, too, but then her phone rang and everything stopped. Like a cold blast of air had come flying through the room."

"Who called?"

"Etta."

"Ahhh." Ari's "I am wise" voice rises to greet me.

"I hear that tone. What does 'ahhh' mean?"

I can hear the gears turning as she lines up what to say, and seeing as she's a top-notch editor and a worker of the words, she's going to be able to soothe my worry, right?

"What I see is a woman in denial. You two are comfortable to the point it's weird to think about crossing the line because she knows she could lose you if things don't work out or thinks she could push you away if you aren't interested, too."

Women. "This is all so complicated."

"Welcome to relationships 101. My thought is that you need to either go out on a proper date with her or be a cavalier dum-dum and try to make her jealous instead."

Could my baby sister be right, that all I need to do is talk to Dylan myself? I'm willing to bet she is; it's the sane and logical idea, really, but also the one that scares me the most. There's an ease in just staying status quo sometimes, isn't there?

Taking a deep breath, I know what I have to do: I need to get Dylan alone so we can talk. Really talk, so I can clear the air, or at least my side of the street.

"Okay." I take another spoonful of ice cream. "Maybe I can see if she wants to meet up tomorrow night early to talk."

"Good!" Ari squeals with glee. "You guys have a shift tomorrow night?"

"No." I pause, connecting the dots of what I'm about to say. "We have a date."

"Huh?" I hear Ari spit out whatever she's drinking on her end of the phone. "A date?"

"A double date, kind of." Even with Ari screeching in my ear, I manage to fill her in quickly on the scenario, wrapping it up with the fact it was Zac who forced my hand.

"This is a mess. You know that, right? You've gone from having a nice talk to 'making her jealous' in one conversation." I can almost see her expression as if she is sitting beside me. "You're going on a date with your roommate, who you do not want to date your best friend, but she's trying to set you up with your boss's sister. Do you follow?"

Oh, I do. Only too well.

FIFTEEN

Dylan

It's hard to believe we've gotten so much done in only a few days' time. Dad managed to get in touch with a local realtor the other day, and she had emailed him a list of things we needed to get started on doing around the house. All tasks that need to be done if it's going to be ready for viewing soon.

Boxing things up and preparing to move has also given me plenty of alone time to think about my own bad choices I've made lately. As I'd crawled into bed last night, Reid had texted, telling me he and Zac had a better idea for our group outing and asked me to check out Culture Shock's latest post. I'm not sure if it's super strange or super cool that they had the same idea as Riley.

To say I'm having reservations about going tonight is an understatement. Saying yes to going on a date with someone I'm not interested in, at all, just so I can bear witness to the man I'm in love with on a date with the woman I'm setting him up with...because I'm too weird?

I can't even roll my eyes any longer, it hurts too much. I've spent a lot of time in eye-roll land today as I've packed up.

"We're really making good progress on this place. I'm willing to bet we can get it on the market in the next two weeks."

Spinning on one heel, I find Dad standing in the doorway of his bedroom with his hands on his hips, looking at all of the boxes stacked neatly around the living room. Only my spin lacks the grace and style that a ballerina would have. I'm like a small elephant caught between cardboard boxes. My little spin goes off the rails when my right leg hits one of the boxes stacked beside me, throwing me off balance and into the giant box meant for our television.

Above me, there is only chuckling. "You okay?

Opening my eyes, I find my father staring down at me. My sweet dad. How do I tell him no, I'm not okay. I'm actually a mess. A mess lying in the middle of the living room who doesn't think she should get up because if she does, it means she is physically okay and that she should go out tonight.

I could also say I'm so not okay because I'm pushing the person I'm in love with straight to someone else because I feel like my life is too complicated to wrap him in at the moment.

Or I could just keep it all in.

Smiling, I take the hand he holds out, allowing him to help me up. "I'll be alright. That's what I get for trying to add some flair to boxing."

"You've done a great job, sweetie. We wouldn't be this far along if you hadn't been so focused the last two days." Helping me to my feet, his eyes scan the room. "It's so organized!"

Each box is clearly labeled; I've inspected them and made sure they are in order and for once, when it comes to this move, I'm feeling on top of things. Mostly because I want one of us to be in the position to keep things moving forward with so much static and undercurrent happening for my dad.

He may think he's hiding it, but I can tell his ego and his

pride are taking a hit with this. To be at his age and have to sell your house to keep your business, well, that's one thing. But to not even know if that money will end up helping in the end is ludicrous in my opinion. What I wouldn't do to get ahold of his old accountant. And slap him.

But, instead, I'm here now, helping my poor dad figure things out again. Scanning the room, I nod in agreement. "It's going to be ready for the realtor to take photos by the end of next week, easily." Pointing to the boxes, I flick my wrist like Hermione would if she was casting a spell. "We can get the boxes stacked on the right to storage, and all of the boxes over here"—I point to the other side of the room where more boxes flank the opposite wall—"all of those are yours to go to your new apartment."

Dad looks around, his smile fading when he realizes my boxes aren't anywhere to be seen. "And where are your things?"

I tip my head toward my bedroom. "Some are there, some are going to storage."

The shadow that falls across his face makes my heart dip. "I'm sorry, Dylan. I'm so sorry that my issues are forcing this on you. I never meant it to get this far. I honestly thought I could fix it, but with the banks not willing to back a loan... well, the writing is on the wall."

Hearing the strain in his voice, I hurt more. I know it's hard for him. The fact he was able to pick up and leave California to move here and start over, that was a big deal. He'd bought a house, started a business, and was thrilled he could start working part time in the fire department so he could still be around his first love, cars.

The fact this is happening now is devastating. Not only to him, but to me because I have to watch my strong, amazing father go through it, and I feel like I have nothing to offer. Man, I feel like a broken record.

"I'm going to find a way to help you. I swear to you, I will. If I have to get full-time work doing something that's temporary but can bring in relief, I'm on it." Throwing my arms around his neck, I squeeze him like only a little girl can do to her father. "We'll figure this out somehow."

"I don't know what I did right that I got you as my daughter, but I'm glad I did." He won't look at me, but I can see the wet on his cheeks.

"Well, you don't have to worry about me living with you at the garage, you can settle in there and take it over on your own. I'll be a temporary roommate."

"Have you found a place to live?"

I can't tell him no, because I don't want him to worry about me. But the fact of the matter is that Max and I can live out of a suitcase if we need to.

"No, but I'm on the hunt for a place and for more work. I applied to be full time at the Sweetkiss Creek station, so that would come with a pay raise that I can pitch in with, you know, to help." I hold up crossed fingers. "So we'll see what's in store next for me and Max."

Hearing his name, my little terrier appears at my feet and looks up at me with expectation. Scooping him up, I cuddle him close. "No walkies, yet, buddy. But Grandad will take you on one while I'm out tonight."

"That's right, tonight is the date." Dad laughs as he opens the refrigerator and pulls out a can of soda. "Did y'all figure out where you're gonna go yet?"

"I think we're going to go check out the new escape room that opened." I pull out my phone and hand it to Dad to show him Andrew's latest column. "My man says it's the place to check out if you're into challenging puzzles that won't get you frustrated."

"Wow, it's like he's talking to you, isn't it?" Chuckling, he hands the phone back. "I've heard about those places, great for team building, but it depends on who you want to bond with."

I hadn't thought about that part. Was Reid's last minute suggestion to change our date to an activity going to result in his getting even closer to Etta? And that sentence makes me crazy, because essentially what I'm doing is trying to get them together, but now I find myself wanting to create some kind of get-rid-of-Etta spray, like fly spray. Etta repellent, if you will.

I need help. Send help. Lots. And friends who can carry me away and tell me I'm better than this.

Huffing, I throw myself down on the couch. The stark bareness of the room now that so many of our knickknacks and pillows are packed away fits my mood. Even the art is off the walls, adding a layer of bleak to the day I didn't know existed.

Biting on my cheek, I decide it's time to tell him about the other day. I've always been open with my dad, and he is my main man. If anyone can help me see through this, it's him. "I saw Reid the other day, and we almost kissed."

Hairy eyebrows, thick as a Maine Coon kitten's fur, arch straight up his forehead. "Oh you did, did you?"

Nodding, I stare at the floor. "Yeah."

Other women I know would never talk to their dad about this kind of thing, but mine is different. Even when Mom was around, he was the one who took me to play groups, made sure my hair was braided if I wanted it to be, or signed me up for gymnastics or cheerleading or even empowered me to play Little League baseball one summer because I wanted to—I was a great shortstop, by the way.

"Okay, well..." He clears his throat, a light flush of pink creeping up from his neck. "I'm not going to lie, Dyls, if it was anyone else I probably wouldn't be so odd right now, but since it's you and Reid, I feel like I'm invested in this. I don't want to say the wrong thing, honey."

Of course he doesn't, and I understand why. He's the one who has had a friendship with Reid before I moved here and now his daughter is asking for advice around her love life. I wouldn't want to be him right now, either.

"It's okay. I don't need you to fix it. I just need to tell you in case you have some advice for me." Looking at my watch, I sigh and push myself back up to standing. "Especially since I'm about to be locked in a room with him for an hour. I'm going to get a shower and get ready to go."

I'm almost across the room when a stray pillow flies past my head. Knowing I've packed them away, I turn around to find my father hunched over the box marked "pillows" pulling another one out so now he holds one in each hand.

"Hey!" I point to the box. "I just finished packing them."

"They won't break," he says with a chuckle, holding one high over his head. "Now, you're going to listen to me for a second. Do I have your attention?"

"Okay!" I hold my hands up in front of me in mock surrender. "I'm listening."

"I'm not going to pretend like I know what's going on, but do whatever it is that will make you the happiest. I don't care if that's kissing Reid or dating his friend, moving to Europe or flying into outer space, I just want to see my baby girl happy. Capiche?"

It only takes me two seconds to cross the room and throw my arms around my father.

"Thank you."

"You bet. Now go, get ready for your big night out...and wear riot gear."

Laughing, I manage the energy to roll my eyes, hopefully for the last time today. "Dad. You don't need to wear riot gear to an escape room."

SIXTEEN
Dylan

I should have worn riot gear to the escape room.

From the moment we met in the lobby, it was clear to me that at least two of us were not going to be bonding or team building anything today. In fact, if we get out of here before the bomb goes off, we're all gonna be lucky.

"Give me that." Etta's voice is clipped as she swipes the second clue from Zac's grasp. From the word go, these two haven't seen eye to eye. At all. It began when Zac asked who would wear heels to an escape room after looking directly at Etta.

Needless to say, she didn't appreciate his attitude very much.

"Let me guess, you're a fan of the Dallas Cowboys aren't you?"

I'm aware that Reid's head is spinning as much as mine as we watch these two go at it, and I'm pretty sure we could both use a bowl of popcorn for this. The good thing about Etta and Zac not getting along is that I've been so busy trying to be the peacemaker, I've not allowed myself time to get all awkward and uncomfortable around Reid.

It's also meant that having to make small talk is definitely not happening here tonight. Which is a win for me, since I'm sure Zac is a nice guy. But he's just not the guy for me.

Glancing at my watch, I see we still have at least twenty minutes to go. Twenty very long minutes until we get out of this room.

The Lock and Key escape room is like nothing I've seen before. When we arrived, we were briefed in the sparse lobby, and given our instruction: there's a bomb that is set to go off, but the villain has locked us in his office, so we can't get out and disarm it. Our mission is to find our way out of the room so we can stop the bomb from being detonated and, basically, save the world.

When you're let into the actual escape room, this part is set up like you're entering someone's office. It's dark, no windows, with bookshelves lining one side of the wall. There's a huge banker's desk in the middle and the room's filled with filing cabinets, computers, plants, a couch...all the office essentials one would need plus a good deal of clutter. Because apparently villains like clutter.

Undeterred and on a mission, Zac continues poking around cardboard boxes, digging inside them for clues. "Oh, I love the Cowboys, sweetheart. Been a fan since I was little. How did you know my family's from Texas?"

"I didn't." Etta's snippy tone is heavy. "I guessed by the accent you're trying to hide. Embarrassed of being brought up in the backwoods?" Etta slams her hand on her hip, and I move around her, opening drawers and poking through plants still in search of our next clue. I want to rally these two. My eyes find Reid's and he looks at me and throws his hands in the air, not sure what to do, either.

I try a different tactic. I tap on Etta's shoulder. "You guys, we don't have much time left..."

But it falls on deaf ears.

Zac, who had been digging around in the trash can, cries out as he stands up. He holds a set of keys in one hand, ones I feel could be used to open a certain drawer I can't get into right now. As he jingles them, he taunts Etta.

"Aren't you a peach? One of these Southern women I hear so much about. All class and proper etiquette and all that jazz?"

"Peach?" Etta snorts, swiping at the keys. "I'm from the north. Here's a hint...I'm a fan of the Washington Football Team."

"You guys!" I reach in between them and grab the keys from Zac's hand. I need to stop this back and forth before I suffer from whiplash. "We're supposed to be working together to get out of here. Not being mean to each other because we wore heels or don't like the same teams."

Two pairs of eyes snap to mine, but Etta is first in letting her guard down. I watch as her shoulders start to slide back down to their normal position. Beside her, Zac lets out a huge breath, his eyes rocking over to Reid's.

Reid clears his throat and takes the piece of paper out of Zac's other grasp. It appears Zac has somehow ended up holding on to all of our clues so far. "We're never getting out of here unless the arguing stops and we get to work, guys."

"We'd have been further along, but someone insisted that we try to find the first clue on the desk and not look under the rug like I wanted to." Zac reaches over and takes the keys back from me and dangles them in front of Etta. "I think we have a banshee in here. Did they want us to find a banshee in the escape room?"

"Aren't you the one who wanted to look under the rug?" Stomping her foot, Etta takes a step toward Zac. "Oh, that is rich. You wanted me to pull the books off the bookshelf and see if the clue was hidden in there. Do you know what a waste of time that would have been?"

Turning to Reid, I nudge his arm. "We should just signal for them to let us out. I don't see how this can get any better."

Taking a step closer to me, he hip-checks me as he leans down so only I can hear him. "If you'd just let me finish what we started the other day, I know we could make this night a whole lot better."

I can no longer make out Etta and Zac's arguing, just static where words once were. There is no one else in this room right now; it's only us: me, Reid, and his big beautiful lips.

Feeling a small sweat start at the base of my neckline, the awkward sensation I hoped to avoid surges. My mouth is dry, and I think I forgot my name. Something sliding across my hand makes me jump in surprise, but when I look down and catch Reid's fingers snaking across my skin, a thrill releases inside me.

But, we're not alone.

"Oh, come on! There is nothing there, Etta, you're wasting precious time."

Zac's exclamation makes both of us snap our heads toward the insane pair to see what's happened now. I'm shocked to find Etta on her hands and knees by a desk that's in the corner of the room, peering underneath it.

"Shush, hand me your phone and turn the flashlight on, please." She holds her hand out and we watch as he slips it to her. She shines the light under the desk, then crawls out a moment later looking triumphant. "There's a safe under here!"

Reid holds up the slip of paper with a series of numbers on it he commandeered from Zac. He hands it to Etta. "Then this must be the combination."

With a whoop of joy, she throws herself back under the

desk, elated and entertained, while Zac stands next to her insisting he's the reason they found it.

I'm trying to stand next to Reid and not want to reach out and press my lips on his. I'll stand here and tell myself I don't need a "him" in my life, someone whose strong arms can and will catch me when I need them to. Who needs anything that awesome?

Me. I do.

I want the awesome, I can see the awesome...heck, I almost tasted awesome on my lips the other day. Now, I need it like flowers need sunlight and fish need water. Now, in this room where we're stuck with the Bickersons, I know I need Reid.

"Argh!" Etta stands up, her mission under the desk an obvious failure. "I think the combination is here to throw us off. It's not working."

"Did it have a lock on it, for a key?" Pointing to the keys in Zac's hand, I offer a solution. "If so, maybe one of those will work."

Clapping her hands with glee, Etta snatches them from a surprised Zac's clutches and, kicking her heels off, is back under the desk. We hear a few odd sounds, some bumping and scraping, but in a few seconds she cries out in delight.

Crawling out from under the desk for the second time in five minutes, she waves a manilla envelope in the air. We huddle around her as she opens the tab, pulling out a handful of documents that are stuffed inside the package.

As we lean over her shoulder, someone has come up behind me and is leaning into me. I can tell it's Reid from the pattern of his breath. I feel the heat of his body pressing into mine, and I fight my own primal urge to lean back into him like a cat in heat.

What is wrong with me? One tiny touch from him, and I'm wasted. I'm like a moth drawn to the fire. I want him, but I can't. I don't think I'm good enough right now. Definitely not in a position to be girlfriend material. Look at how complicated things are. I have to take care of my father right now, and I don't want Reid to feel like he's hooking up his boat to a sinking ship.

Looking at Etta, she seems put together and good, she has a big heart and definitely has some Reid-like ways to her. It feels weird to me to even think about it, but I have to be okay with it because I'm also really starting to like her. And I am not and will not ever be the kind of woman who hurts a girlfriend over a man. No way, no how.

So for now, I'll take the feeling of having Reid pressing up against me while I remember our almost kiss. But Reid has other ideas. His fingers are back, tracing tiny lines up and down my right arm, my skin rippling with anticipation. Closing my eyes, I wish I felt different, that it was just us in this room. But it's not.

"Look!" Etta screams, jumping in place and thus shaking all of us out of our spots, forcing us to take a step back. Which also meant I had to step away from the warmth of Reid, and back into the cold.

Etta holds a sign in the air that says "CONGRATULATIONS." She spins around, waving it around in sight of the various cameras angled on us, where the escape room workers that are watching us for safety have been sitting this whole time. Swallowing, I'm curious how much they watch and see, because tonight they would have gotten their money's worth, that's for sure.

Everyone high-fives, getting along for a brief moment because hey, we cracked our code. In a matter of seconds, a bell sounds and a bookshelf on the other side of the room swings open. Etta and Zac try to squeeze through the doorway at the same time, with Zac finally relenting and letting Etta go first.

I follow them and turn around, finding Reid standing alone in the middle of the room with a funny look on his face, watching me. Even with this small distance between us, there's a hum of life, zapping back and forth, my body knowing he's there and responding in kind. It's the smile playing on those lips of his that knocks me, that beautiful perfect smile that hurts my heart.

Because I want him to be mine.

SEVENTEEN

Reid

Watching Zac and Etta argue over who solved the last clue and which one of them needs to be exalted? Exhausting. It's like watching two people bring out the worst in each other, over and over again. In one very tiny room that looks like someone's dark, dingy study in England.

I'm glad we made it out alive, but I am man enough to admit I wanted to be in there alone with Dylan at the end. I shake my head, trying to get the thought of how soft her skin is out of my mind. I'm thanking my lucky stars that when Ari and I did this escape room thing a few weeks back, well, when "Andrew" tried it out, I was able to experience it the way you should. I'm as competitive as the next guy, but today was, simply put, a dumpster fire.

When the door, or rather the bookshelf, had opened at the end revealing the tiny cafe, I was flooded with relief and pure longing. Longing to hold Dylan? Yep. Exchanging a look with her, we leave the tiny room and make tracks to the first empty table we see and sit down, taking chairs opposite one another.

"I told you I had it under control." Zac slides the chair out beside Dylan and sits, crossing his arms and staring at Etta, who takes the chair next to me. "I'm pretty sure I told you to try the keys out when I first found them."

"Really?" Her voice is taunting, like a small child who knows they're right because their parents have always told them so and because they are, indeed, always right. It would be kind of funny if I wasn't so worn out. "So now you're Scooby Doo, huh?"

Dylan slaps the table with her right hand. "I'm going to go get a chai latte and something to eat. If anyone wants anything, speak up. I'm treating." She points one bony little finger at me. "Should I make it two chai lattes with almond milk?"

Out of the corner of my eye, I notice that Etta stops paying attention to Zac, turning in her chair to face me but keeping her gaze on Dylan.

"Chai latte with almond milk?" Her head swivels back and forth between us. "Is that your usual drink, Dylan?"

"Love them. Got used to them when I was on the west coast and now I'm an addict. They are my kryptonite." Smiling, Dylan nods as she stands and grabs her purse. "I even got Reid to start drinking them instead of having so much coffee all the time. Do you want one?"

"Actually, I think I'd like an iced coffee," Etta says at the same time Zac pushes his chair out and hops up beside Dylan.

"Hey, let me." Zac grabs his wallet from his back pocket. "My treat."

"That would be sweet." Something in Dylan softens. She smiles and waves a hand over her shoulder as she walks away. "Come on."

As they head toward the counter to order, I turn in my seat to find Etta is now looking at me, with a big old dopey grin on her face.

"Chai latte, huh?"

Confused, I cock my head to one side. "Yes. Why?"

"When I saw you that day at the firehouse and we talked about your favorite drink, you went on and on about how much you loved chai lattes." Etta dips her chin, crossing her arms in front of her chest, her eyes rocking over toward the line. "Are you into the chai or the gal?"

Now Etta's in my face questioning Dylan, like everybody else does? I'm super thrown. Thrown across the road and under the bus kind of thrown. "What are you talking about?"

"Please. I know that you know exactly what I mean."

I could come clean, but not yet. Not here and not to Etta. My eyes rock over to the counter where Dylan stands with Zac, laughing at who knows what, and I feel a prick of jealous heat deep inside me.

Looking back at Etta, I take a deep calming breath. I'm prepared. "I am into the chai, I'll have you know."

"Oh, really?" she says, doubt dripping from her words.

"Did you know there are several types of chai one can have?" When Etta's mouth drops open, I'm spurred on. "Tulsi chai, which is known for using the herb Holy Basil, and there's Bombay cutting chai whose flavor is quite strong and served usually in half doses. There's also ginger chai or Adrak as it's also called. And Masala chai, which is my personal favorite... just to name a few."

Etta shakes her head in disbelief. "You've got to be kidding me."

"Nope. I told you. I love chai." And I also listened when Dylan explained all of this to me ages ago, when she was sharing her love of chai, but Etta doesn't need to know this.

I'm prepared to deep dive around the spices involved with making chai, but thankfully Zac and Dylan are back from placing our order. Dylan's eyes bounce back and forth between me and Etta, watching us like a hawk. Wanting to keep things peaceful around us, I change the subject and fast.

And sometimes, in love and war, changing the subject means you get some casualties.

"Zac is a quilter." I think I just had a stroke.

"Huh." Dylan tilts her head at one angle, then to the other side, squinting her eyes and looking him up and down. "I don't get the grandma-vibe from you." She winks as she nudges him with her elbow. "That is pretty cool, though. I'm not very good at sewing, crochet, knitting...any of that."

"My nanny taught me how to do it when I was little, and I've kept it up as I got older." Zac stretches his hands in front of him, studying them before he looks up and winks at Etta. "Gotta keep my mitts perfect, you know."

"The fact you call your hands 'mitts' tells me everything I need to know." Etta rolls her eyes and turns in her chair so her back is half to the table. I'm getting the feeling she may be one foot out the door, too.

"Well, I think it's cool that she did." Dylan smiles at no one in particular as a server appears and places our drinks in front of us along with a small plate with a few sweets on it. "You had a nanny?"

Zac nods, his cheeks blushing. I know what these two don't—that Zac is from *the* Wright family in Beaufort. They're not just any family, but one of the founding families in that area of South Carolina. Zac doesn't need to work if he doesn't want to, but he chooses to, which is alright by me.

I look over to watch Dylan, catching her eyes as they flit across me before she turns her attention to Etta. She grabs a tiny cupcake off the plate in the center of the table. "What's going on with the tasting room idea? Any movement there?"

Etta shakes her head. "It needs a lot of work done if we're going to set up at the campground, and Amelia doesn't have the resources to back it as a project in the immediate future." She shrugs as she picks up her glass and brings it up to her lips. "I'm going to meet with her tomorrow so we can go over options. I really want that location now that I've seen it."

"Who knows?" Dylan takes a sip of her drink, placing it back down on the table in front of her. "You could end up finding an investor."

It doesn't escape me that Dylan is trying to not make eye contact with me. I keep looking, pretending it's like we're playing Pacman and I'm one of the ghosts chasing the little yellow guy around the board. Once I get her attention, I know I only want it on me. Which feels selfish and narcissistic, but you know what? I don't care.

I've sat quietly for so long wanting to be hers. The one who sits next to her, like Zac is doing tonight, only I know for sure he won't be getting a kiss with a promise in it at the end of the date.

"A tasting room?" Zac scoffs as he leans across the table to pluck a treat from the plate. "At a campground?"

I can sense Etta about to snap. The big hint happens when she smacks the table with both of her hands.

"Yes. A tasting room at the campground, you troll." She picks up her hands and shakes them in the air. "Ouch, that hurt."

"I wasn't making fun," Zac says defensively, looking at me with a question in his eyes. "I'm just curious why there'd be a tasting room at a campsite?"

"You are impossible!" Etta snaps before she sips her iced coffee.

The next few moments are in super slow motion, but will be etched in my mind for the ages. Zac, reaching over to take a cookie off the plate, snaps his hand away at the same time Etta leans forward to put down her drink. There's no time to cry out a warning nor time to react; instead, all Dylan and I can do is watch it all unfold.

As Zac's hand connects with Etta's iced coffee, which also

has a scoop of vanilla ice cream, the glass slams onto its side and spins in a circle. At first, the spinning is so fast the gravitational pull keeps the liquid inside, however, as it slows down, ice cream, coffee, and whipped cream bits are spat out of the glass, the contents managing to find their way onto all of us.

Carnage. Dylan tries not to laugh as she wipes whipped cream off her cheek, while Etta sits in horror, her mouth slung open and pure fury dancing in her eyes, aimed at Zac.

He looks at me, ice cream plastered on the front of his shirt, and shrugs a shoulder. "Ooops."

"Thanks for giving me a ride home." Dylan clicks her seatbelt into place and faces forward, still careful to not make eye contact with me for too long.

"I seriously would have been fine walking home," she insists as she takes her phone out of her bag. "Let me text Dad so he knows I'm on my way back. Now that he's dating, I don't want to..."

The thought scares me. "You don't need to say another word. Text away."

She punches at her phone for a second, then tosses it back in her bag and sits back in her seat, letting out a ginormous sigh. "Wow. That was—"

"Such an interesting night."

Finally, we let it out. We both throw our heads back and laugh hysterically. I've got a tear in my eye, and I'm pretty sure Dylan just snorted.

When we're both done, the collective weight that had been sitting in the car seems to have lifted somewhat.

"Hey, Dyl, can we talk about the other day?" I tap her shoulder lightly, worried she may take off running away from me if I push too hard. "I really want to clear the air with you."

"I have something I need to tell you, too." She turns slowly, so she's facing me. Her eyes are downcast, staring at my hand on her arm. She nods her head and swallows.

This is good. Positive! We're moving forward. I feel like things are going to be different. We've got this, and I'm about to be in making-out heaven. Tripping in the land of lips on lips and kisses for miles. I'm ready to pull her into my arms and finally feel what it's like to kiss my best friend.

Dylan shifts in her seat, dragging her eyes up slowly to finally meet mine. "I don't think we should be anything more than what we are."

"Huh?" It feels as if someone has taken a sledgehammer and rammed it into my gut. "I'm struggling here. What do you mean?"

"I think we should honor our friendship, and just simply be that." Her arms cross her body and she hugs herself tightly. "Good friends. The best, but not with—benefits."

Surely I'm not hearing this right. This woman has rewired me, she's reworked me, and made me hers over the years. She's pulled me apart and put me back together again...I am all Dylan's.

"Why are you saying this?" Resisting the urge I have to scream, instead I focus on her fingers. Fingers that dance across her anxiety ring, spinning the small beads. It's her tell, at least as far as I'm concerned. I know when she does this, she's feeling flighty. "Dylan, we have a connection. Some days I feel like everything begins and ends with you...but you're happy to be just friends?"

She looks down again, beyond her hands to her feet. The inside of my truck gets smaller; I feel like we're being cinched closed as she nods.

"Etta seems like..."

"Stop it." I grip the steering wheel and shake my head.

"You've been going on about me and Etta. I'm not concerned about Etta."

Reaching out, I put my hand on her arm. Chestnut brown eyes meet mine, void of their usual golden flecks which sparkle like a caramel sunshine when she's happy. Instead I see only sadness in their reflection.

"I'm sorry, Reid." Dylan's eyes flicker as she watches my hand on her arm and sighs, closing her eyes as she does. "Please don't ask me to try to explain right now. Just trust me."

Trust her? Haven't I always? That's what's led us here.

Her energy shifts and she turns to look out the window. Keeping my eyes on her, I wonder what I have to do to get inside that mind of hers and convince her that I'm the one. I'm her person.

But I know her and I know her well, and we'll not get anywhere now. So I do the only thing I can right now.

I take her home.

EIGHTEEN

Dylan

When I pull into the parking lot at the dog park, I'm thankful all is quiet here on this sunny Sunday morning. In the last couple of weeks it's gotten increasingly busier, which is great for Max and socializing my sweet angel, but when you need a place to think and chill...well, I want a park bench overlooking some dogs running and playing happily and to do this solo. Is that so wrong?

Unclipping the leash from his black harness, I watch Max take off in a silver streak, racing down the hill to meet up with the four other small dogs who are running around their fenced area. Finding my favorite bench empty, one where you get a great view of the whole park, I jog over to it and claim it for mine. My mind is spinning, and I need to slow the ride down for a little bit.

I think back on recent events: preparing to move out of my home, trying to find new work—and, sadly, my recent application for full-time work being rejected by the Sweetkiss Creek fire department. I've pushed my best friend away—who I'm in love with—toward another woman, who at least has become a friend. All because of my own insecurities about money and the way Reid sees me has me tied up in knots.

No wonder I'm exhausted. I wear myself out.

Telling Reid a few nights ago after our double date that he needs to be with Etta was just the weirdest thing I could have done. Ever. I don't want him with her, I want him with me. I want his lips to be on mine, I want to feel the heat coming off his warm body when he holds me close. The thought makes me shudder and a cold flash reverberates through my system.

First things first, I need to tell Andrew my thoughts on the escape room adventure. Can I put "would have rather it been called the disappear room" because maybe one of us would have been pulled away into some alternate life universe that night instead of the insane commotion we called a double date?

Staring at the screen, I type out a few comments, finally deciding on "Four out of five stars, would have been five but then I would have had different teammates." Hitting send, I feel like I'm at least being honest. Andrew isn't someone who judges me or knows me; he has no clue who I am just as I have no clue who he is. He's probably the one person in the whole Love Valley area who I could talk to right now about my issues with Reid and he'd get it because he's not really involved. Third party contribution, I like to call it.

My phone beeps in my hand. Looking down, I'm surprised I've gotten a response on my comment—and it's from Andrew himself!

A. Jenkins: Uh oh. Someone wasn't happy with their escape room partners?

It's not like he hasn't answered me before. It's just the first time we're online at the

exact same time. I can see a green dot glowing by his name, proving this to me. Taking a sip of my coffee, I wonder if I can explain my life story to Andrew in three sentences and get his take. He seems to be an even-keeled kind of guy, if how he writes is any indication of his personality.

Puppylover915: Four of us went. Two weren't happy with each other. But we had fun.

Andrew Jenkins: Four of you went. How was the other person, the fourth? Were they not having fun, too?

Puppylover915: He's the kind of person who always has fun wherever he goes, so yes. He had fun in the escape room.

Andrew Jenkins: Sounds like a nice guy. But, fun people usually are.

I turn the phone at an angle in my hand. Is Andrew Jenkins lobbying for Reid? Shaking my head at the absurdity, I look around and spot Max still running gleefully at the same time I see what looks like Etta's car pull into the parking lot. My stomach dips. We've not seen each other nor spoken since our night out. Not ready to talk, I go back to my phone, which is buzzing in my hand again.

Andrew Jenkins: Anyway, we have good news for you. You're the one thousandth comment on my posts for the Lake Lorelei News Post! We're planning a special event for a meet and greet with a few locals. Since your name was chosen, you can bring a plus one.

What? I won something? A tiny squeal of glee erupts from deep within me before I can clap a hand over my mouth or think sanely. My happiness has now alerted Etta that I'm here, and she's waving at me like one of those inflatable men you see at a used car lot. Wacky waving arm men.

Waving back, but not in a wacky way, I point my nose into my phone once more.

Puppylover915: Really I won? That's so cool! I'd love to come.

Andrew Jenkins: Awesome! Someone from the paper

will email you soon. Very casual evening, but we're looking forward to meeting you in person.

I stare at my phone, a little elated and super excited. It buzzes one more time.

Andrews Jenkins: Can't wait to meet you.

"Hey you." Etta slides onto the seat next to me, throwing an arm around my shoulders to give me a hug. "I was hoping to see you soon to download what a crazy train wreck the other night was. And to apologize for any part I played in it."

"You definitely don't need to say you're sorry for a thing. I think the stress came from the intensity of having to solve a puzzle in an hour." I shrug my shoulders and try not to laugh. "Sorry, I'm trying to give you a pass."

"Oh, I know." Etta sighs, throwing herself against the back of the bench. "Zac just made me so crazy! What a know-it-all."

"Maybe he was feeling a bit competitive with Reid that night, since it was a game and all that."

"Or just competitive with him in general." If Etta's eyes were fingers, they'd be tickling my whole body right now as she sweeps them across me. "Or maybe there was a prize they think they need to compete for? Although, if that's the case, then Zac is just a jerk who was taking out his competitive drive for something he can't have."

I cock my head to the side, confused by Etta's words. "But Zac and Reid weren't the ones arguing."

"No, but do you think Zac is going to fight with his friend and his new roommate?" She laughs, pointing to her chest with both thumbs. "It had to be me. I was the outsider to them that night."

Shaking my head, I lightly tap her hand. "No, you weren't. You were Reid's date."

"No. I wasn't."

"What do you mean?"

"I need you to do something." Etta opens her purse, rifling

through it. Her hand pops out a moment later holding a mirror. "Look at this."

Opening it, I see myself. My skin is glowing from both the heat of the day and the coffee warming me from the inside. My hair's a mess, and I need sleep. I hand the mirror back.

"Thanks, you've just reminded me I need to get my roots done."

She shoves it back at me. "Look again."

I do. When I cut my eyes to look at Etta, she's smiling. "That's the woman Reid wanted to be on a date with."

Snapping the compact closed, I hand it over again. "Stop it."

"We both know that you two are head over heels in love with each other. I figured it out before the date, but I had to still go through with it just to see if you two would."

"What?" I can't stop shaking my head, it's like I'm trying to wake up at four in the morning after an all-nighter without mainlining espressos. "But, you've been asking about him."

"For my friend back in D.C. who is single and amazing, but she's not the kind of gal who wants to be the third wheel." Etta giggles. "You two are made for each other. So my advice is to stop trying to set him up on dates he clearly doesn't want to go on and try talking to him yourself."

I wish it was as easy as she makes it sound. I really do. Do I want to tell him I'm in love with him and want him to be my forever? With everything in me, I do, but when I think about the changes I need to make so I can assist my father, my family, I can't help but feel like I would be dragging him down.

"I'm not having the best of luck lately." Sighing, I turn and angle my body to face Etta. "I didn't get a job and it's one I really need. I don't just need it so I can afford my own place, I need it because my dad needs my help."

"What do you mean?" she asks.

"If we're not making the payments to the IRS they

require, every month and consistently, starting next month, they'll take his business away. They've already got him selling his home, which is the reason we're moving out." I stare out at the park. "The kicker is that I just got out of my own debt recently and had squirreled away money for savings. I wanted to use it as a down payment on a house in the future."

Etta shakes her head. "And you can't keep it?"

"I could, but I'm going to give it to my dad. He needs it more." Spotting Max running along the fence line, I manage a small smile. "I'll figure it out, I always do. I can't have him losing everything he has at his age, when I know I can rally and pick up the pieces."

"Oh, wow." Etta's hand covers mine in a show of support. I'm sure it counts that I already liked her even when I thought she liked Reid, but having the weight of her hand over mine in such a vulnerable moment is everything right now. "I knew there was something happening but didn't realize you had taken so much on."

"I wouldn't want to have it any other way, though. He's my dad and he helped me, so it's my turn." Scraping the toe of my Converse in the dirt, I stare at my feet. "I just wish I could find a miracle. Housing and a job."

"You know, you do have an option." Etta leans in and nudges me with her shoulder. "Amelia."

"Amelia?" Seeing as I'm still getting to know her, I hardly think I can ask Amelia for help or a loan of some kind. I shake my head. "We're not that close, so I can't ask for a loan."

"Not a loan, silly. Remember when we were at the campground the other day, she mentioned she's looking for a manager?" Etta's smile widens as she holds out her arms. "Ta da! Why can't it be you?"

Thinking back to the conversation, I feel something shift inside me. "I hadn't thought of that. I mean, I guess I could be?"

"You won't know unless you talk to her. Reid told me about the experience you have with events; don't you think that could come in handy if Amelia's also hosting festivals and other big events at the campground?" Her eyes flash with excitement. "Seriously, this is soooo good!"

Her excitement is contagious, so much so that I find myself reaching for my phone and pulling up my last text to Amelia.

"Why not?" I can think of a million reasons why, but none as to why not. But one does come to mind, causing me to hit pause on my text. "But what if it's so full time I can't be a paramedic any longer?"

"Dylan!" Etta grabs my phone from my hands, tosses it to the bench and grabs both of my shoulders. "We've not known each other for long, but I hope we're on a friendship track. And it's because of that I'm going to do you this favor and tell you to stop it. Stop overthinking everything. You must feel like you've run a mile by ten in the morning every day if this is how you operate."

She's got my number. "Pretty much."

"Okay, as your official new friend, our first task is to have you text Amelia and ask for a meeting, then we'll get you prepped for it so you can walk into that meeting and wow her to the tune of getting what you need." Etta tucks my phone back into my hands. "After you send that text, we're going to talk about you and Reid."

Taking the phone from her hands, a tiny flutter hits my chest. The kind you get when you realize you've got a friend—one you can tell is going to be a good one. Here for the lifetime, not the reason nor the season.

I suck in a deep breath, type out my note to Amelia, and hit send, pleased when she texts back a time and an address for us to meet the very next day.

Showing Etta, she grins. "Well, let's go prep."

NINETEEN

Reid

When the front door to my parents' home swings open, I'm surprised to find my sister behind it. I know she was the one who talked me into coming over here today and telling them my good news, but I had not expected an audience.

"Step into my lair." Using her hand in a sweeping motion, she ushers me inside. "I got here about an hour ago. Figured I could be your warm-up act."

She jerks a thumb over her shoulder, indicating to the kitchen table behind her, and I smile. There's a huge pink box on it, which I know is from their favorite bakery, and it means that box is stuffed with croissants, regular and chocolate, and Danishes.

Closing my eyes, I sniff the air. "Smells like coffee, sugar, and...do I detect a hint of bad choices?"

She nudges my shoulder. "You forgot sprinkled in one little white lie, but to be fair, it's one for the greater good."

"I hate calling it that." I really do. I hate having the word lie associated with me in any way. "It's a secret identity. A nom de plume I took on in order to be my best self."

"Who taught you nom de plume?" Ari asks, arching an eyebrow so high it almost pops off her forehead.

I nudge her shoulder back and give her an exaggerated wink. "Research. And I watch *Wheel of Fortune* sometimes. It was there, Pat Sajak explained it all."

We're both startled when the door to the living room suddenly flies open, my father standing there with a croissant in his hand along with my mother.

"I'm sorry, but did I hear you say that Pat Sajak is giving you kids an education now?" My mother may be a petite woman, all of five feet and two inches, but she can make her presence known.

"Not so much an education." I kiss her cheek and give her a squeeze. "Just filling me with more useless trivia that makes me question why we need school to begin with."

Dad steps forward, croissant in one hand, to pat my back as he breezes past me for more coffee. "I hope that's a joke."

Making sure only I see it, Ari rolls her eyes and sticks her tongue out, but gets everything on her face back in order before either one of our parents sees.

"Daddy, of course he's joking." Ari wraps an arm around his shoulders, proving her status as "clearly the favorite," a role which she tries to deny. Look, I'm fine with it. Every family has one, right, so let it be me who paves the way for her to be the golden child.

"We can't tell with you kids anymore who's joking and who's just sarcastic by nature." Mom chuckles as she pours a refill into her coffee mug, holding the pot in the air. "Want a cup, Reid?"

Nodding, I smile in gratitude, watching as my father pulls out a chair and sits down at the table. Taking a cue, I do the same and watch as Mom and Ari follow suit behind me.

"Well, this is clearly a surprise for us to have both of you show up, randomly, on a Friday morning." My parents exchange a look across the table.

"The croissants are one thing, but sweetie"—my mother turns to Ari—"is everything really okay?"

Laughing, Ari reaches into the pastry box and picks out a strawberry Danish, plopping it on a plate in front of her. "Can't we stop in to say hello to our parents together on the same day?"

"Yes—but you don't." Dad's eyes rock back and forth between us, finally landing on me. "We've not seen you in weeks and you work down the street. Your mother and I were about to issue a formal invitation to get the two of you over for dinner at the same time."

"And now here you are, at our table, with food." Mom punctuates the sentence by pursing her lips and giving us *the* look. You know, the one only a mom can give when she's seeing right through you because she's the one who brought you into the world and the one who can take you out of it if you buy into that kind of thing. I do. Like I said, my mom is mighty.

Taking a big breath, I wrap both hands around the mug of coffee in front of me. "Okay, it's me. I wanted to talk to both of you at the same time, and Ari suggested we—"

"—collaborate." Ari pats my mother's hand. "Because we've done something, together, but the big news is all Reid's. You know?"

"No, I have no idea what you mean." Dad looks at Mom across the table. "Do you have any idea what they mean?"

"No clue." She sips her coffee, waving a hand in the air. "Please continue. Unless you think we need popcorn for this?"

Ari shakes her head. "No, no popcorn needed. It's not drama. It's good news."

"Ahh, I see." My father tips his coffee mug at my mother. "It's slaps, right?"

My head jerks in my father's direction. "Slaps?"

"Yes, sweetie. Slaps." Mom giggles, looking at me like I'm the one who is making up words. Sighing, she rolls her eyes. "Slaps is slang. I learned it at youth group last night. Apparently it's what the kids these days say when something is amazing or really cool."

Ari and I look at each other, neither one knowing how to react. I'm the one who breaks the shock and awe of the silence first.

"Well, okay, then yes. This news is slaps." Turning to face my dad, I incline my head with respect. "At least, I feel like it slaps, if we're slapping now."

"No, dear." Mom pats my shoulder. "It *is* slaps. Not *it* slaps, that's a whole other sentence entirely."

"Oh, wow." Ari sits back in her chair and looks at the ceiling. "To think I passed on a planning session at work for this."

"Let's walk away from the slaps convo and come back to why I want to talk to you both." Drumming my fingers on the table, I sweep my eyes around the room and make sure I've got everyone's attention.

I've been waiting over a year to share this news, and I finally get to tell them. My heart races, to the point I freeze. I am frozen and cannot move. What if I kept this secret all this time and it really isn't a good thing? What if they hate me for doing it? Here I am thinking I'm delivering good news to them, but what if my dad thinks it's just not good enough?

Why has my brain decided now is the time to bring up every insecurity I've ever had as a son at this very moment?

Ari must have sensed some hesitation on my part, so thankfully she steps in. "So, you know how that column Culture Shock, the one in my paper, has been taking off?"

To my shock, my mother's eyes light up with pure excitement. "I love that Andrew Jenkins! He's got the best insight around things to do, but it's his writing that keeps me entertained." She smiles, tapping the table to make sure she has my father's attention. "Mike, remember that article of his you liked? The one about the art gallery that opened."

My dad arches a singular eyebrow, much like the signature move of Ari's. I know where she gets it from. "Yeees. Why?"

"You said how much you liked his voice." She pushes herself back from the table and takes her plate to the kitchen sink before returning to sit down again. "I distinctly remember you reading that column to me. We both got a kick out of it."

His eyes flash with recognition. "The same guy who wrote about that corn maze, right?"

"Yes, that maze was insane!" She winks at my father. "Remember he wrote 'be careful what you say when you're in the maze...'"

"'...because it's all ears.'" My dad guffaws, a sound I don't think I've heard come from him before.

"Yes, that's him." Ari, who is leaning back in her chair, laughs along with my parents as she points across the table in my direction. "Like, seriously. That's *him*."

My parents, who are still laughing, follow her finger, their sights landing on me. They laugh a little harder with my mom being the one whose laugh begins to taper off as she realizes what Ari's said is true.

"Wait a sec." She looks at my dad, who's also caught his breath. "Are you saying that Reid wrote those articles?"

I hold a hand in the air. "Guilty. It's me. Hi. I'm Andrew Jenkins."

"You?" My mother's mouth hangs open as she waits for confirmation.

I give it to her in the form of a nod, shrugging my shoulders. "Surprise?"

I haven't looked at my dad yet, but when I do, I'm a little confused. He's not reacting, at all. If we were measuring this on a scale, he was at a ten until I told him I was Andrew, and now he's gone to...we'll call it a three.

There is literally no expression on his face. My heart races and kicks, wanting to jump out of my chest and leave. If this is the way he's going to react, how will Dylan take it when I finally tell her? And she's invested in Andrew.

"There's more, though." Ari to the rescue. She looks at me and nods her head in encouragement. "I'll let Reid tell you the big news."

My palms grow slicker and my mouth is dry. Licking my lips, I find I can take a breath. Hallelujah. I slowly bring my eyes up to meet my parents' faces. "I signed a book deal yesterday."

"You what?" My mother is out of her chair and wrapping her arms around me, screaming in my ear. "Now, that, my family, is slaps!"

Laughing, I embrace her right back and hold on, grateful for her reaction. Thankful for her patience with me and really, really loving having my mother say she's proud of me.

"It wouldn't have happened without Ari's support and her vision." I tip an invisible hat in my sister's direction.

"I saw talent and I wanted it, so really it was purely selfish on my part." She walks around the table to stand next to our father, leaning against him. "What do you think?"

His eyes rise slowly to meet mine, and they lock. We spend what feels like an eternity here, but it's only about ten seconds we're suspended like this. I wonder if he can see the perspiration forming on my upper lip. I'm agonizing over how to wipe it while keeping an illusion of being calm, but there's no way.

Breaking our gaze, he sits back in his chair and crosses his arms across his chest. "Why does it matter what I think?'

"Because you're our dad, we want to know what you think of this." Ari grins as she dances in place.

"You." He shakes his head and points one long finger, wagging it in my direction. "Why do you care what I—we—think?"

The question is, frankly, a good one and it's one I've asked myself a lot lately.

"Because I want to know that what I'm doing in this world, with this life you gave me, is something you'd be proud of. Something you'd approve of." I find myself looking down at my hands, turning them over in front of me. I swear I'll probably be able to trace every line on my palm after this conversation is done.

"Our opinion means that much to you?"

Nodding, I keep my eyes on my hands. I think I found my life line, the crease that stretches across my palm connecting the wrist to the forefinger. Shame I can't call a life line right now, but that's a whole other life line, like on *Who Wants to be a Millionaire...*

Oh, wow, now I'm doing a Dylan spinout. I digress and refocus, looking back at my dad.

"Your opinion means a lot to me. I started writing as Andrew so I could have freedom to say what I wanted. I didn't want anyone to know it was me in case I messed up, but when it took off, I decided to keep writing and see where it took me."

"Within the first three weeks of running Culture Shock, our online hits went up over 150 percent." Ari laughs as she reaches over our father to grab another Danish from the pastry box. "Reid has single-handedly created an online hub for our paper, and its flow-on effect for our community is insane. We had a publisher approach us wanting to sign him for a book, using his columns."

"And," I interject, ready to take over now, "when Ari and I

met with them on Saturday to sign the contract, they offered me two more deals. To write two more books."

I don't have to look at her to know my mom is crying, I hear her sniffling beside me. I quickly lean over and kiss her cheek.

It's his approval I want. His words. His reaction. I know my mother is behind me, she tells me all the time, but this about me and my dad.

"Well." His eyes focus on a random spot on the table as he speaks. "This is a surprise. A big one."

Nodding, I swallow. Hard. "I know, but it's also exciting."

"Well, Reid." His eyes make their way to mine, a smile following suit. "It's definitely slaps."

I'm not sure which one of us is out of our chair first, all I know is that I'm hugging my dad and do not want to let go. I mean, we do, finally, but it takes a minute. Not going to lie, I think we both choked on a tear or two.

As we all sit back down, my mother holds up her coffee mug. "To our kids. We're always here for you, no matter what you do or who you become. We're proud of you."

Mugs clink together as we mark the moment, and my father taps my shoulder.

"One thing I want to get out into the open is that I am always proud of you, Reid. I don't care what you think, I am." His lips twitch as he fights a smile. "I could see you getting nervous to tell me your good news, and I don't want you to ever be scared to tell me, or your mother, anything. As long as you're happy in this world, with what you bring into it with your energy and your heart, then we're going to be right here supporting you."

It's my turn to fight a small tear. Nope there's two. I've got two tears, one in each eye. I quickly swipe at my right eye, but my mom must have seen it, too, because she passes me a tissue.

Pressing it to my other eye, I look at my dad. "I always thought I was letting you down."

"How? By being a firefighter? " Dad shakes his head. "By being a firefighter in training, who also managed to go to community college and get an associate's degree while holding down a part-time job?" He looks at Mom, who rolls her eyes. "Honey. He thought I was let down."

"I told you that you needed to call him more." As she says this, she kicks me under the table. Snapping my head in her direction, I see her fighting a smile, too. "There is nothing in this world you two could do to make us stop loving you or to feel let down. Period. The fact you two ended up banding together to do this, now that is something we need to discuss because, wow, that is powerful!"

"Oh, thank goodness you didn't say slaps." Ari laughs, tapping her watch. "Because it's not going to be slaps for Reid if I don't get him to his next appointment."

"Ahhhh." My mother is a little bit too all-knowing about this one. "That appointment."

"The one about Dylan?" Dad pipes in as he swipes another croissant for himself. "I guess if you're out there clearing the air, you need to make sure the love of your life is in on the secret, too, right?"

"How do..." I look at Ari. "Did you tell them?"

She shrugs. "No more secrets in this family, plus they asked."

"We're invested, sweetie." Mom gets up out of her chair and stands beside mine. "We are, and have been, Team Dylan from the moment you two met."

"This is so weird." I push my chair back, Dad doing the same, and my parents escort me and Ari to the front door. "Am I really that transparent?"

"I know what a man in love looks like, son." Dad wraps his arms around my mother, pulling her tight against his chest.

The smile on her face tells us there's no place else she'd rather be. "Women love grand gestures. Go out there and get her, and when you finally get her to say yes or to be all in with you, make sure you spend every day trying to make her smile."

Looking at the two of them in front of me, I have hope. I turn to my sister and pull my car keys from my jacket as she holds up her hand to high-five me.

"Let's do this."

TWENTY

Dylan

Having good news to share is the best feeling, but it can feel like Christmas when you get to tell the absolutely fabulous, oh-so-good it hurts news. My favorite part is seeing the expression on someone's face change once the words are out of your mouth.

Like now, when I'm sitting here looking at Riley and watching her face morph into hundreds of micro-expressions because I've just shared my good—no, great news with her.

"You're going to be running the campground for Amelia?" Riley repeats for the third time. "That's awesome! I can't believe you topped it by also getting the house as part of the deal!"

"I know!" Throwing myself on the couch beside her, I can't help but feel light, like a weight is beginning to come off that needs to be shed. "I told Amelia I'd be happy to find a place to live if she wanted to rent the house out, but she'd rather have me on site so I'm there for any issues."

Riley hops up from the couch, shaking her head in disbelief as she crosses the sparse room. With almost everything now gone, either in storage or at the apartment over the garage, we are two days away from getting the house on the market. The couch, a coffee table, my dad's old record player, and a selection of his favorite albums remain.

Riley slides one of the albums out of its jacket and places it on the turntable. "Do you still get to work part time on the ambulance?"

"Yes, but funny enough I have news about that, too."

As "Lucy in the Sky with Diamonds" hums to life, Riley grins, waving her hands in the air. "Did you know this song has four meanings? It's been said it's about John Lennon's mother, about LSD, about someone Yoko met who called themselves a savior, and I read where it's a response to a drawing Julian Lennon made for his dad, John."

This is why I love her. If I have to play trivia with anyone, this is my partner, ladies and gentlemen.

Riley shakes her head, as if she's shaking away her thoughts, and comes back to the sofa. "So what's the other part of your epic good news? I don't think I can take much more."

"I'm leaving the Lake Lorelei Fire Department."

"What?" Her jaw drops open. "Does Reid know?"

"Not yet. I'll still be on the roster and available to fill in, but I'm taking a part-time role in Sweetkiss Creek. I applied for a full-time slot recently and they said no, but then they came back to me last night and asked if I'd consider part time." I shrug, grinning. "I hate leaving because Lake Lorelei was my first gig, but it makes more sense for me to work in Sweetkiss Creek now that I'll be living down the street from the fire-house there."

"Wow." Riley's eyes are wide. "Are they paying you more?"

"Oh, you bet they are."

We both fall into the couch giggling, Riley kicking her legs in the air above us. I'm sure we look like two bugs that have fallen on our backs and are too round to roll back over and be right-side up, but I don't care.

"Oh man, enough excitement. My heart can't take it." Breathing a sigh of relief, I sit up and smooth my hair back. Glancing at my watch, I tap it. "I still can't believe we get to meet Andrew Jenkins tonight."

"I still can't believe you're so excited to meet this blogger," Riley says with a giant smirk on her face.

But I can't get mad about it, and I won't defend the columnist, not today. I'm too happy. "I'm gonna let that one slide, due to circumstances being what they are...but I will remind you that I need you to be nice. I bet he's some nice older guy who's studied journalism for years, and he probably lives and dies by some writing code."

"You say older, and I think he's, like, in his seventies." Riley laughs, clapping her hands together. "But, would a seventy-year-old have tried out the new skating park last year?"

I think about it for a minute. "Good point. What if he's a kid?"

"And you've been crushing on a teenager this whole time?"

I make a face. "No way. There was too much experience in those articles to be written by someone who hasn't fully lived life yet, not that teens don't live life...but you know what I mean. Worldly experience."

"I feel you." Riley is up and back over by the record player, exchanging the Beatles for Supertramp. She replaces the vinyl, one for the other, then turns around to face me, cocking her head to one side as she looks me up and down. "So, Reid?"

My stomach sinks. The one person I need to talk to is also the person I'm most nervous about seeing. "I don't know what to do. When I saw him the other night, I basically said I wasn't interested and he should look elsewhere."

"Maybe you can try explaining to him why you've been so crazy? You guys are tight, and I see him watch you. I know he loves you because it's written all over the poor guy's face." Riley points to my planner on the coffee table. "That thing, your life bible? He got you that because he knows you love being organized."

She grabs my hand, looking at my anxiety ring. "And this? A Christmas gift one year? Puh-lease. I remember seeing him the day he ordered it. Did you know he asked my opinion on it?"

Well, that's a surprise. "He did?"

Riley nods in her all-knowing way. "Wanted to make sure you'd like sterling silver over gold. For the sake of all things you hold dear to you, have you not noticed he orders the same exact drink that you do, a chai latte with almond milk, of all things?"

"Well, yes, but I turned him onto those, so of course..."

"Open your eyes, Dylan!" Riley slaps her forehead. "You're the girl who doesn't see that her best friend has fallen for her, and if you don't step up and tell him you feel the same way, you could lose him."

Riley then gasps, clutching her chest. "Do you realize that you're actually, like, in one of those rom-coms you love so much? Except it's the one with the miscommunication trope."

I wrinkle my nose. "Oh, I hate those."

"Right? I'm always looking at the screen and going, 'Hey, dum-dum, he's right there! Go get him,' you know?" She places a hand on each of my shoulders and looks deep into my eyes. "Hey, dum-dum! He's right there!"

"Okay, okay," Laughing, I pull away, but yeah. She's right.

"You were worried because he was your partner at work, right?" She throws a hand in the air. "Well, you're leaving the Lake Lorelei fire department, so that won't be an issue. Next problem?"

"I didn't like the fact I wasn't…" How do I share this part of me? "Riley, this one hurts to say out loud, but I was embarrassed that I wasn't 'financially packaged,' I guess?"

Her face twists in surprise. "Financially packaged? What are you going on about?"

"I was ashamed, Riley. Sure, I look good on the surface, ticking all the boxes, but when I moved here, I was paying off a huge debt and didn't want to saddle anyone with that. Then once I got out of that hole"—I sweep my arms around the empty room—"all of this happened to my poor father."

"What does it have to do with you and Reid, though?"

"My pride?" Shaking my head, I realize how hollow the words are. "My ego? I didn't want to show up in front of him, waving my hand and saying 'let's date' when I'm falling apart behind the scenes."

"And now, you have a plan." Riley reaches over and grabs my arm. "You said your dad is even dating now, and look at what he's going through. If you find the right person, you can work anything out and weather all the rough stuff together. Just be open. There's no shame around any of this. Don't you think it's time for you to be happy now?"

"I don't know, Riley."

"Dylan." The emphasis she puts on my name tells me she's over it. "It's as if you think you're not enough, but you are. You, my dear, are perfect as you are. I feel like you show the world this laid-back Dylan version of you so we think you're cool as a cucumber, but"—she taps my chest—"there's another one in there. It's the Dylan your anxiety brings to the surface. She's the one who worries about not being a complete package."

I open my mouth to protest, but Riley beats me to it, holding her hand up to stop me as she continues. "You are the complete package, and guess what? The right man has seen it. Now it's time for you to let it happen. Give yourself permission to be happy. You left your world in California to come here and help your pops out when he needed it. You're ready to drop everything for him, again, and loan him the money you've been saving to buy a house. You're pushing your needs aside and stepping in to help because that's what family does."

I can only nod my head and let her words wash over me. Riley leans over and squeezes my hand. "Go. Go look in the mirror and pat the woman you see there on the back, because she's amazing. She's got flex and she's rocking some superpowers, we just need to remind her every now and then, cause we all get lost sometimes."

Hearing the words spoken out loud is like a blast of cold water to your naked body on an even colder day. I want to see Reid and grab him and hold him close, but I also want to kiss those lips that keep sneaking their way into my thoughts. I can see the curve of his top lip and imagine myself placing my mouth over his, getting lost in him and his kisses. Just thinking about it, my skin prickles. I'm taken back to the moment on the dance floor when he wrapped his hand around my waist and pulled me tight to his body, so I could revel in every curve.

I'm thinking bad thoughts, and when I look at Max, it's like he knows. He covers his little face with his paw and goes back to sleep.

Of course I get to be happy, all I want is to be happy. But I'm realizing I've spent a lot of time being really ridiculous, too. The room is filled with the sound of a record that's come to the end of its song. Sighing, I stand up and walk over to turn the record player off, Riley following suit as she grabs her purse and car keys.

"I need to go and get things done today." She puts her arms around me and hugs me close. "I'll meet you back here tonight and we'll go to the venue together, okay?"

Wrapping my arms around my friend, I don't want to let

go. I'm blessed that Riley's in my life, and at this moment, I'm so grateful she's on my team.

Even if it is Team Dum-Dum.

TWENTY-ONE

Reid

Walking up the sidewalk to the garage, my heart slams so loudly in my chest, I'm pretty sure Dubs will hear it coming before the rest of me is inside. I know that before I do anything else today, I need to make sure I talk to this man about an idea I have.

I'm surprised it's quiet; Dubs usually is in the garage tinkering away with an engine or he's underneath one trying to fix something. His car shop may be one of two in the area, but he's the best of the bunch. He always finds time to look at your vehicle and makes each person who enters the premises feel like they're number one, and I'm pretty sure he's donated time and parts before if someone hasn't had the funds to cover the cost of something.

As I walk past an old Ford Mustang he's rebuilding, I smile, knowing this car is one he wants to give to Dylan one day. She doesn't know it, but I do. I remember when he bought it at an auction the month before she moved here. Said he was getting a project he could work on to pass down to his daughter one day, the idea being she'd then pass it on to her children.

I stop to admire the car, which has no color except patchwork as it's had so much done to it over the past two years. But the hood is smooth, and just touching a car that I know is going to have a V8 dropped into it gives me a buzz. Because I'm a guy and this is the kind of thing we love.

Which is one of the reasons why I'm here.

"She's a beauty, isn't she?"

Dubs's sarcasm isn't lost on me. He must have been in the office; I never heard him walk up. Grinning, I turn to face him and pat her hood.

"She's gorgeous. How much more work do you need to do?"

"I'm hoping by next year, summer, she'll be ready." He shrugs, leaning against the other side of the hood. "This is the project I use to let go of my other problems with, and seeing how many of those I've had to navigate lately, I may be done sooner."

The worry lines, by now, are deeply etched into Dubs's features. Looking around the garage, I just can't accept that it would be sold out from under him, nor can I accept the fact that no one is able to help him.

"You need something, Reid?"

Bushy eyebrows shade his eyes, not allowing me a glimpse of what he *may* be thinking. My palms are slick with perspiration for the second time today and my stomach is in knots, more knots than anyone could ever tie on a rope, and don't ask me how long that rope is because in this case, it's miles.

"Yes." Swallowing, I stand a little straighter, making sure my button-down shirt is tucked in. Dylan is always nudging me to dress a little nicer, so I figured why not start today?

"I have a proposal for you," I begin, but the way Dubs's eyebrows fly to the top of his forehead, I'm feeling like I'm setting the wrong expectation. I mean, we'll get there—I do want to talk to him about his daughter—but something else comes first. "You probably know or would have figured out that Dylan told me about what's going on."

"Oh." His playful and chipper expression is officially wiped from his face, and he casts his eyes down to stare at the floor. This isn't the Dubs the world needs. "Yeah, Reid. It's an ugly situation, and complicated, but I know I'm going to figure it out."

"That's why I'm here." Nervousness takes over, so I shove my hands in my pockets. Sometimes, when I'm nervous, I wave my hands around a little wildly. Don't need that little tick to appear now. "I've come into some money lately I wasn't expecting, at all. In fact, it's pretty overwhelming."

"Congrats?" Dubs laughs. "Sounds like you're nervous about spending it, but as Dylan would say, you need to just go 'thank you, more please', and wait for the universe to deliver." He chuckles, shaking his silver hair side to side. "She's so L.A."

"That's the thing, spending it feels weird. The whole thing is weird, but it doesn't matter. What does matter is that I have money and I want to invest it somewhere." Now's the time to unleash my hands to do the wild talking, so I do. I let them out and they sweep the air around us. "I want to invest in you. In Dubs's Garage."

A myriad of emotions register on the older man's face as my words sink in. The final look is one of confusion as he shakes his head, again.

"What are you talking about?"

"I mean it, Dubs. I know you think of me as this kid from the fire house who is always trying, maybe messing up sometimes, but I feel like I have a good heart." Winking, I treat him to my cheesiest grin. "And here you are, the dutiful and professional older fireman who has been around the block a time or twelve."

I realize I may have pushed that too far when he says, "Did you just say I was older?"

Swallowing hard, I try not to flinch. "Yes, sir."

He crosses his arms in front of his chest. "And do I look like I've been around twelve blocks?"

Yes, I definitely pushed too hard. Note to self, learn to shut up, Reid. "No, not at all."

"Okay, as long as we're clear." He waves a hand at me, indicating I can keep going.

"Anyway...your garage is more than a place where people bring their cars. It's vintage touches, like the old Texaco sign you have on the wall, the waiting area you created with darts and a pool table, the same space where I've come to hang out with Dylan before to play a game when my car wasn't even in the shop."

Dubs looks around the garage, a gleam in his eyes. "I wanted it to be the ultimate man cave, but I never got around to adding the oomph I wanted for it, you know?"

Nodding, I step around the car, closer to him. "I get it, and I see your vision for it. So much that I want to invest in the garage so we can first get the government off your back, then second, make it the man—and woman—cave you intended it to be."

His face, once again, has a plethora of emotions washing over it. It lands on the one where his mouth hangs open and his jaw slams to the ground.

"What did you do, man, rob a bank?"

"Not quite, but I have signed a deal that has pretty much set me up for a solid few years." And I'm not lying; after I'd left my parents with Ari, we'd stopped by her office so I could review and sign my other contracts for the publisher she'd gotten the deal with in New York.

Bless my little sis, she's acting as my agent now, but don't worry. She'll get her ten percent.

Dubs squints his eyes as he looks me up and down. "I sense you want to tell me what it is, but you can't?"

"There is someone else I want to talk to about the deal first, then I'm happy to tell you, but til then, I need you to trust me. If you don't mind getting your paperwork together with all of the debt that is owed, I'd like to sit down with you in a day or two and go over it. We can decide together the best way forward."

"You really want to do this with me, knowing the trouble I'm in?" Dubs is back to that confused look, accompanied by a side of shaking his head. "It's a lot to comprehend. You understand, Reid, that you are instilling so much trust in—"

I hold a hand up. "Let me stop you there, Dubs. There is no one else I trust more in this world, besides my parents, of course, and Ari. You've been beside me as we've run into burning buildings. You trust me in those circumstances, and I trust you. I know that the debt you owe is one we can take care of together and make it so you can breathe easily again." I put my hand on his shoulder and squeeze. "I want to do this for you, but also for me. For me because it's an investment in myself, and the future I hope to have, as well."

Dubs tries to angle his face so I won't see the tears welling in his eyes, but I see them. "Did the waterworks start because I touched you?"

"Yeah," he snickers, wiping a tear away. "Your touch is like magic."

"So, what do you say?" I hold out my hand for him to shake. "Partners?"

He looks at my hand, then slowly starts to put his hand out...only to snap it back at the last minute. "I want you to know if you see the dollar amount and it scares you, we can reassess."

"It won't scare me, but fine. I agree." I keep my hand out and wait for him to link with it, but he hesitates again.

"I can make payments to you for the tax debt."

"I wouldn't have it any other way."

"Deal!" Satisfied, he wraps his hand in mine and pumps my hand up and down enthusiastically. "Oh, Reid, I don't think you know what you've done for me. And for Dylan."

"That's the other reason why I'm here."

"Dylan? Boy, I cannot encourage you more than I already have to ask her on a date or do whatever it is you kids do these days...go out, check a box yes or no. I don't know, just please, would the two of you figure it out?"

"I've figured out that I want her and you know how much I care about her already, so—"

Dubs cocks his head to one side, listening. "You okay, Reid?"

"The two of you are close. So close. I know you've been her only man for a long time. Because of that, and because I know what my intentions are, I wanted to ask you for permission."

"Permission?"

"I'm not going to ask her today, and it won't be tomorrow or even next week. But sometime, very, very soon I plan on asking Dylan to be my wife."

A grin flashes across the older man's face. "Son, you need to ask her on a date first. Shouldn't we start there?"

"I could, but I'm banking on the fact she says yes to that first date. I hope from there, we're exclusive and it doesn't take too long to get there because we know each other already. She's my best friend, and I know that I only want to make her happy for the rest of her life."

Dubs gives me a thumbs-up. "Well, then, what are you doing here? Would you go out there and get the girl finally?"

TWENTY-TWO

Dylan

"Are you sure the email said to meet here? At Wings of Glory?"

Without even looking, I reach into the center console and grab my phone. Signaling to turn right into the parking lot, I hand it over to Riley, who's sitting in the passenger seat, scratching her head.

"I thought the same thing." Don't get me wrong, Wings of Glory is a good place to eat in town, but there's nothing super special about it. Well, besides the fact that Wings of Glory has been the place where Reid and I have gone pretty much every week since it opened—and since Andrew wrote about it.

Peering through the windshield at the shopping center in front of us, I can see movement inside the main windows of the restaurant. All of the lights are on, but from what I can see there's not a lot of people inside.

"Let me see that again, please." Holding out my hand, I wait for Riley to put the phone in it, but she doesn't. She does keep her eye on the restaurant, though, craning her neck trying to see in.

"Hey." I tap her shoulder. "Can you hand me that? Maybe I read the directions wrong."

When Riley turns to me, her face is etched in pure glee but in an evil way. Not evil, like Lord Voldemort evil, but best friend evil. The kind of evil where I know something is about to not go as planned.

"What is that look for?"

Riley stretches her Cheshire Cat grin even wider before she slides my phone into her purse and opens her car door. Getting out, she leans down to address me before she slams her door shut. "Get out, Dylan."

I have never seen her like this. Not one to argue, at least not with Riley, I do as I'm told, walking to meet her at the front of the car. She holds out her hand.

"Keys." When I hesitate, she taps her palm. "Now."

"What the..." Begrudgingly, I put them in her hand. "I hope you have only good intentions for me, cause I'm nervous now."

"That's the last emotion you need to feel right now." She takes a good look at me, straightens some stray piece of hair and tucks it behind my ear, then hands me some lip gloss. "Put a bit of this on."

I take the tube from her hand and slide the cotton candy pink gloss across my lips, my eyes bouncing over to the restaurant. "Call me crazy, but this seems a little over-the-top for a meet and greet."

"Crazy," Riley says with a wink. She then turns me in a circle, as if inspecting me, patting my butt and giving me a little shove. "Alrighty then, away with you. Get in there."

Confused, I turn around and face her, snapping my head back to look at the venue. "I thought you were coming in with me?"

Riley shakes her head. "This is as far as I'm going tonight."

Crossing her arms, she tilts her chin toward the shopping center. "But someone is waiting inside for you."

Still not sure what's going on, I turn back around to see what she's looking at and my breath leaves my body.

"Reid?"

Reid

I've been waiting for this moment for way too long. Watching Dylan through the tinted windows of Wings of Glory, my heart bangs against my chest. I'm afraid it's going to crack my sternum or send me into cardiac arrest, it's that intense.

As she opens the front door and steps in, I can feel her hesitancy. And no wonder I went through the wringer organizing this surprise. I'd like to blame this whole surprise scenario on someone else, but this was all my idea.

When she'd commented on Andrew's post the other day, I happened to be online replying to comments at the same time. We hadn't spoken at that point since the escape room, and I'd done nothing but think about her since we left.

I honestly do not know what it is that came over me; I only know that I saw her name pop up. Good old puppylover915. When she wrote she'd liked the night out but wished she had other people with her, I wanted to type "ME TOO, BOO!" but I refrained.

Instead, I made up a contest on the fly. One that she's the only winner of, but she doesn't need to know that. No, I made sure I got Ari onboard to help me secure a location for Andrew's "meet and greet,'" also known as my grand gesture. Then I kind of filled Riley in, knowing she is the best girl friend and someone who I also needed to get onboard to help get Dylan here.

Riley also made me feel better when I questioned the fact that Wings of Glory might not be the best place for a grand gesture. Then she reminded me how it's Dylan's favorite place, because of me, and I knew we were onto something.

Now, seeing Dylan looking so befuddled and beautiful? I'm in love.

I watch as she looks around, allowing her eyes to get adjusted to the darkness of the interior.

Holding up a hand I wave. "Hey, Dylan."

"Reid?" Her head tips dramatically to one side, and she looks around again. "What are you doing here?"

Threading my way through the empty dining room, I start walking over to where she stands. "I'm here because I wanted to see your face when you got to meet your favorite writer."

Crossing her arms in front of her chest, she shifts her weight to her right side. "Really? But Riley was supposed to be my plus-one. And she's outside acting weird."

Slowly, I keep walking, but I take my sweet time.

"That's because I didn't want her to come inside." There it is. The look on Dylan's face I hoped for, and if I'm correct, this is phase one of three. "I wanted to have you in here alone with me."

"You what?" She laughs. "What are you talking about, Reid?"

"Did you ever notice how Andrew's articles always have a little something in them that you feel may have been written just for you, a sentence or a tidbit of some kind where you feel connected?"

"How did you know that?" Her mouth quirks as she watches me. "I must have told you that I felt that, right?"

"Did you ever feel like any of the columns he posted were written to bring you pure joy?" Left foot, then right foot...I'm still working my way over to her, but I'm dragging it out.

Testing the actual science behind a "slow burn" at this very moment.

She shifts her weight to the other foot. "Kind of, but that's the sign of a good writer, isn't it? That they can put the reader into the picture with them and take them on a journey."

"True." Only a few more steps and I'll be standing in front of her. "But, I need to know what you would do if you found out those articles were written by someone who was only thinking of you the whole time they did it?"

Right foot, left foot. She's watching me, her breath hitches. Maybe she's putting it together, maybe she's still confused. One more step, then around the last table, and—

I'm here. Standing in front of the woman who has, can, and will make me my happiest and my craziest in life. She pulls those golden-chestnut eyes of hers up to meet mine, searching.

"Reid," she whispers as she holds a hand out like she's trying to stop me from coming any closer. "I don't understand."

"It's me. I'm Andrew." I pull my eyes from hers, the surprise being a little more than I can handle. Staring at my feet, I continue. "I've wanted to tell you this for so long, but things are happening now where I *have* to tell you."

"What?" Dylan's hand flies to her mouth, punching back a tiny squeal when she does. "You're Andrew?"

"Yep." I shrug and give her a little bow. "I'm sorry I didn't tell you sooner, but I wanted to make sure it worked first. I didn't want to tell anyone because if it failed, if I failed, then I didn't have to own that it was me, you know? It's my insecurity and it was stupid."

Dylan's jaw has gone slack, her eyes wide. "You're Andrew."

While I have her silenced with shock, I step in and take her hand, lifting the back of it to my lips before letting it go so I can tell her about the book deal, or rather (let me clear my throat) my book *deals.*

She listens intently to the whole story before reaching over and taking my hand in return. Her eyes flit across mine as she gently strokes the inside of my wrist. It takes me a moment to realize her fingertips are dancing across my tattoo.

Slowly, Dylan smiles and pulls her eyes away from mine. She stares down at the artwork on my arm. "The fact you have something inked on your skin that I helped you pick out should have been a sign, huh?"

"I think we both know that we've been fighting our feelings for a little too long now." Using my thumb and forefinger, I bring her face closer to mine and tip her chin so I'm looking right into her eyes. "I don't know about you, but I'm over it."

The smile that covers her face tells me she's over it, too. Dylan's hand touches my face gently as she cups my jaw and leans in closer, the heat of her breath slamming into my mouth.

"I'm so over it, that I've got nothing left except to be here, right where I've always wanted to be." Her forehead touches mine. "I've been making up excuses for a long time as to why I shouldn't be in love with you, Reid Shannon, but I've run out. I'm tired of exhausting myself by overthinking. For once, I want to stop thinking and just take action."

"I like action," I growl, letting one of my hands find their way around her waist, pulling her even closer to me as her fingers thread their way through my hair. I let my gaze travel along her earlobes and down to her decolletage, and it takes everything inside of me to fight the primal urge to nibble on her neck, especially the area right behind her ear and at the base of her hairline—I want to send shivers racing across her body like I have on mine.

Instead, I drag my focus back to her lips, those beautiful, perfect tiny parcels of beauty that wait for my kisses. But it's her kisses I need more than I need life itself at this moment. It's her kisses I've waited for for so long, the kisses I want to wake me in the morning and the kisses I want to be the last ones I receive at night.

Dylan's fists pull on my shirt, tugging me in close to her, and my mouth closes on top of hers. The warmth, the softness, the inevitable thrill that races through me heightens my awareness of her to no limits, not that I want any.

Her lips press into mine, and I allow myself the time to explore, wrapping my hand in her hair and pulling her into me. She's ready for the exploration as well, pressing back harder and wrapping her arms around my neck, in what I hope is as much an effort to steady herself as it is to steady me.

As she makes her way down, fingertips dancing along my chin, then fluttering hands moving along my arms and coming to a rest on my forearms, I pull away breathless and hopeless.

Hopelessly in love, that is.

Big brown eyes slam into mine, smiling. "Hi, Andrew. You can kiss me anytime."

Laughing, I do as instructed before pulling her into my chest and squeezing her close. "Are you sure you aren't disappointed that I'm Andrew?"

"What?" She pulls away, smacking me in the shoulder. "No way! Now, I know who he is and get to ask him questions. And hopefully help him when he needs to go and check out new places that open."

"Are you volunteering to be my plus-one?" I ask, kissing her forehead.

"Yes, please," she says with a giggle as she comes in to plant a kiss on my lips.

"Good, because we'll have a new but old business we'll need to check out soon. I got wind that a local favorite is getting a new investor. They're probably going to have to plan a grand re-opening just to introduce the business to the community."

Dylan clutches my hand. "Oh, and what business is this?"

"It's a cute little spot called Dubs's Garage." Taking one finger, I trace a line on the back of her hand. "Dylan, I'm investing in the garage and going to back your father. He's not going to lose the garage—at least, not while I'm around."

Dylan snaps her hand back, using it to cover her mouth as she kicks back her chair and stands up, in obvious shock. My stomach flips—this isn't the reaction I hoped for. So, I wait. I watch as she paces around the table before she finally turns to me with her hands on her hips.

"What does this mean?" Her face is mock serious. How do I know? Because I do. "You and my dad are business partners now?"

"Well," I say as I stand up and make my way over to her, "it's going to be a family business. So it only makes sense I'm the one who invests."

"Oh, is it now?" She tries to hold back her smirk, but she can't. I love it. I love her.

"Like I told your dad, just today, one day we'll be family, so I want in now." Taking her hand, I drag her back into my arms, wrapping her tight and pulling her close. Her softness melts into mine. "I wanted to show you that it's me, Dylan. It's always been me and I want it to only be me. And I am all in. Now, it's your turn." Stepping back, I put a hand on each of her shoulders and bend down so we're eye to eye, nose to nose, forehead to forehead. "I need to know, Dylan Williams, are you all in, too?"

The grin she flashes my way is all I need. She does a little hop before throwing herself into my arms. "Whether you ask me tonight, tomorrow, or thirty years from now, there is nowhere else I want to be and no one else I want to navigate this world with but you. I'm all in."

When her lips find mine, it's then that I know we've done it: we've both mastered the art of falling in love with your best friend.

Hmm. Maybe I should write a book about it.

Epilogue

REID

"So when you tell me you're doing research, is it always going to be this amazing?" Dylan asks with a giggle, crossing her arms in front of her chest as she peers out the windshield of my truck. "Because I've been feeling horrible about your late nights at the computer, but now I don't know."

I follow where her eyes are tracking as she takes in the view in front of us. Opening the driver's side door, I hop out and jog around to her door, pulling it open.

"Here you go, my lady." Using my right hand, I make a giant flourishing gesture, sweeping my arm out as if clearing a path for my girl. Holding out my other hand, I dip my head. "If you'll do me the honor, I have a surprise to show you."

Dylan tosses her auburn locks over her shoulder, narrowing her eyes playfully as she looks at my outstretched hand. "A surprise?"

I nod slowly, hoping she'll just come with me. Trying to surprise this woman has been near impossible. "No questions. Just come with me."

Chestnut-colored eyes––full of so many questions––zip up to mine. Biting her lip, probably in an effort to not crack a smile, she slides her hand into mine and climbs out.

"Fine. With a view like this, who wants to talk anyway?" She turns her head, looking inside the truck and pats her leg. "Well, come on Max. We're not rolling out the red carpet for you."

Did I also make sure Max was able to come with us today, so he could be here for my big surprise? Oh, you bet I did. Grinning, I watch as she snaps the leash on his collar and stands up, facing me.

"Let's make the most of this gorgeous place while we're here."

Looking around at the scene in front of us, I know what she means. We'd spent the majority of the day driving around to, for real, finish off a story I've been working on. Well, actually two stories...but the thing is, I know how one of these stories ends.

The other? Well, let's just say I need to be the one asking the questions.

Our first stop today was the Love Valley Botanical Gardens. I arranged...well, rather, Andrew arranged a private tour for us there at the famous Butterfly House. We spent the morning learning about sixty plus different species of butter-flies and learning how to create a DIY butterfly garden for ourselves. After that, we spent an hour driving on the Blue Ridge Parkway, stopping off at a popular overlook and walking its accompanying trail so I could snap photos for my column.

I'd picked the perfect day for our excursion––midweek, not many tourists around even though it's summer. A quick glance at the gorgeous woman beside me and I know she's in heaven as much as I am.

"Wow." Dylan turns around in a circle, looking around us. The words uttered are an exhale, not so much formed for sound. "So this is Chimney Rock?"

"It is." I point toward a trail on the other side of the parking lot from where we stand. "But that's where we're going first. That trial takes us to Hickory Nut Falls."

Dylan looks down at her shoes, then back up at me. "You're lucky I wore the right footwear today and that we brought poop bags. I'm not saying it's not been a good day, but you never told me we were going to be so active."

"You love it," I growl, wrapping an arm around her waist and pulling her hard into my chest. Inclining my head, I tip her chin and lift her lips to mine so I can kiss them.

"I do, but I love you more," she giggles, pulling away and tugging on my hand as well as Max's leash. "Come on. The sign says it's about a 45 minute round trip walk. Let's do it."

Not one to argue, I follow where she leads. It's something I'm prepared to do for the rest of my life. We make our way hand in hand down the trail, passing only three other groups as we walk through hardwood forests by rock cliffs. This area is usually swarming with people, but my timing is impeccable thanks to all of my planning.

We hear the falls before we see them. In my research, I learned that the water flow depends on the amount of rain and usually in summertime, the flow reduces to a small stream. However, timing is on my side and last night there was a huge thunderstorm that came through.

The platform at the base of the waterfalls is thankfully empty when we get there. Dylan lets out a small gasp as she runs to the edge of the decking and looks up, taking in the sight of the cascading water.

Watching this woman, I want to seriously pinch myself. How did I luck out that I got the girl in the end?

Dylan scoops up Max in her arms, burying her face in his fur before pulling back and spinning back around to face me, her smile wide.

"It's so peaceful," she gushes. "Tranquil, beautiful, all of those words that describe nature. I love it!"

Shoving my hand in my pockets, I take a step toward her. "Me, too. It's a special place."

"So this writing project." Placing Max back down on the deck, Dylan puts one hand on her hip as she faces me. "What's the story about again? Is it a tourism write up?"

"It's more than that." My hand grips the small box in my pocket as I begin pulling it out slowly. "This particular column is going to be about the best places in North Carolina for––proposing."

"Ah." Dylan says with a nod, turning away from me only to spin back around as my words hit home. "Wait. For proposing, proposing? Like getting married?"

"That's the plan." I hold out my hand, palm flat with the ring box balanced on it. "And you know how I like to experience what I write about so..."

I'm lucky Max is a good, obedient dog because Dylan drops his leash like it's a hot flare as both of her hands fly to her mouth, covering the tiny squeal that comes out of it. As if he knows his part in today's events, her little fluff ball sits down on his haunches and cocks his head to one side, watching me.

Taking my cue, I kneel down in front of her and open the lid.

"I cannot think of anyone else I want to do life with, it's only you Dylan. It's always been you and it will always be you. I want you to have and to hold through it all." I hold up the engagement ring, an heirloom from my father's side of the family, as I drag my eyes to hers. "If you'll have me?"

Dylan's eyes fill with tears, one even escapes and makes its way down flushed cheeks. She nods, but doesn't speak. I'm going to take it as a good sign and keep going.

"I'm prepared to take Max, too, you know." I reach into my other pocket and pull out a new collar, dangling it in the air. You bet I tried to think of everything. "I need to know if you'll marry me, Dylan. Because if you do, you'll make me the happiest man to walk this earth."

"Oh, wow." Dylan chuckles, her eyes taking in the bejeweled collar swinging on my finger before casting her eyes back to the jewelry box in my hand. The moment she looks, the sun pops out from around a cloud and its light hits the princess cut diamond, sending a shower of sparkling brilliance onto the rocks and decking that surround us. "You pulled out all the stops didn't you?"

"If I need to add any more incentive, I will." Holding my gifts aloft, I bat my eyelashes, making her smile even wider. "So, what do you say? Are we going to be a family?"

"Yes, yes, yes!" Dylan generously allows me the time to slip the ring on her finger before launching herself into my arms, her hands fisting my tee shirt as she pulls me hard against her body. Standing on tiptoes, she brushes her lips across mine. Softly at first, but then with more firmness as she presses her mouth over mine. I feel her heart race, her hands rising up as her fingers dance their way across my shoulder, up my neck and through my hair––gentle tugs sending a thrill across my skin that leaves a ripple effect encompassing my whole body.

Shuddering, I wrap my arms around her and gather her close to me, blanketing her with love while fully surrendering myself to this woman. This gorgeous, amazing, strong, woman who has held my delicate heart in her hands for the duration of our friendship.

And now, I'm ready for her to hold it for our lifetime.

I start to pull away, but can't resist kissing her neck one more time, leaving a trail while making my way slowly up to her earlobe, and allowing my lips to whisper their way across her jawline. Carefully, as if I'm holding a delicate piece of glassware, I allow my lips to brush across Dylan's sweet mouth. I'm so dizzy from this kiss, I need to come back to earth before I crash like an angel who lost his wings. For me, it's mission accomplished. I've got my answer and then some.

It's my turn to scoop Max up and cradle him in my arms while Dylan leans into me, touching her forehead to mine as we both cuddle her furbaby. My wife to be. My step-dog. I've already got a little family...man I'm one lucky guy.

"I love you, Dyls." I press my lips into the top of her head, I simply do not want to stop kissing her but we have to go back sometime.

"I know you do." She pats Max's head before dragging her gaze to meet mine. "I love you too. So much. You've shown me for so long how much you love me." She looks down at the ring on her hand and grins. "I'm excited I get to spend the rest of my life showing you how much I love you."

I wrap one arm around her shoulders and take Max's leash as I set him down and we start our walk back. We're going slower than we have all day, and that's fine by me.

We've got eternity to get where we need to go.

Etta

"Your wedding was the best." Taking my wine glass by the stem, I lift it in the air and smile at my friend. My first real girlfriend since I moved to North Carolina. "May your marriage be one that spans the ages. My wish for you is that you have happiness and good luck in all you do, and that your marriage is the kind that all of us single ladies sitting on the sidelines hold out hope for. It should be..."

"Oy, it should be a simple toast, that's what it should be." Riley might be interrupting my spiel, but she's right. I'm waffling.

Laughing, I make a sweeping motion with my hand as I snuggle in closer next to Dylan. Mrs. Dylan Shannon, that is. "By all means, take it away."

"To you, to Reid, to Max." Riley holds her glass, tipping its rim but being oh so careful not to spill its contents on my couch. "Congrats, doll, I am thrilled for you––and Etta's right, you know. Your wedding was pretty epic."

"It was perfect for being the first one to be held at the new event space at the campground, right?" Dylan's eyes are wide, sparkling with excitement. In fact, ever since she got married this woman glows. She turns and grabs my arm. "And thanks again for setting up the wine pairing with dinner for the reception."

"That was such a great touch!" Riley waits until she's put her glass back down before she claps her hands together with straight up glee. "It was impressive...but so was the donut wall."

"Bonus points that I live right on the property now too." Dylan grins, rolling up the sleeves of her shirt showing off tanned skin, fresh from her honeymoon in the Caribbean. "I swear, working for Amelia is so easy. She's hands on, but she doesn't micro-manage."

"I love that everything seems to be working out for you now." I lean back into the soft goodness of my couch cushions, letting my body relax. I've been going through a lot personally the last few weeks, and I'm not sure if I should bring it up or not. I'm sitting in the safety zone with my girls, where we can let it all hang out and talk about anything, but I don't want to bring the mood down. Not when Dylan is so happy.

"It's only working out because we had nowhere to go but up," Dylan giggles. "Dad's in a good place, Reid's about to launch his book, and I'm...at peace."

"Here, here." Riley holds her glass up again, her infectious enthusiasm bubbling to the surface. If she could bottle that, she'd be a millionaire. "You deserve the best!"

"We all do." Dylan clinks her glass into Riley's before turning to face me. "So, I've had a chance to catch up with Riley but not you and I feel like it's been ages! How are you?"

"I'm doing okay." I try to inject some of Riley's optimism into my words, but I'm failing. My heart is simply too heavy. I know these two women can feel my energy shift, a point which is proven when I look up and catch them exchanging a knowing look between them. "What?"

"Amelia told me about the wine bar, Etta." Dylan reaches over and grabs my hand. "I'm sorry. Is there anything you can do?"

Nothing like having your friends find out about your bad luck and you weren't able to tell them yourself. Doesn't help that one of our friends seems to have blabbed about it, but whatever. I was going to have to tell them sometime.

"I'm going to try getting a loan and if that doesn't work, I'll look for investors."

Riley narrows her eyes, and cocks her head to one side. "What's going on?"

"Remember the wine bar I wanted to open at Sweetkiss Campground? Well, thanks to my ex husband, who is now officially suing me, I'll be lucky if I get the money he owes me for my half of our business. Money which he promised me when I left to move down here, by the way."

The jaws of both women come unhinged as they look at each other then back at me. Riley's the first to speak up.

"How can he sue you? You owned the business jointly, there has to be some kind of law there that says you get what you're owed."

"It's over the IP and set up of the vineyard and our cellar door." Shaking my head, I can't deny the sting in my gut that this particular subject brings. Running a winery with my husband was supposed to be romantic, now it's just a pain. In my butt.

"How can he sue over that?" Dylan throws her hands in the air. "I swear, that's like trying to sue your neighbor because their hedge blocks your view."

"Not the same thing, but I see where you're going with that analogy." Riley nods her head as she grabs the bottle of wine on the counter and adds more to my glass. "I am curious though as to why and how?"

I can only shrug my shoulders. "My head is still spinning, to be honest. According to the lawyer I consulted here, he has every right to do this since we were together and we did it as a joint venture. Even though he didn't weigh in on a lot of aspects of the business, his name is on the paperwork. So, to the law this is fair."

"The law is wrong in this case." Dylan sighs as she crosses her arms in front of her chest. She clicks her tongue against the roof of her mouth. "Look, I don't know who the lawyer is that you talked to, but I may have someone else who could help."

"Really?" Dare I say that I knew it? I knew if anyone could help me, it was gonna be one of my girls. "I'll talk to anyone. Please. Just having to pay out a retainer right now sounds so defeating. I want to get this figured out so I can get on with my life."

"I get it." Dylan grins as she pats my hand. "But the person you'll need to talk to is Zac."

I'm like a balloon when the air is let out. I'm a flower that is wilting in the sunshine because there's no water. I'm a sandwich without bread...I guess that makes me meat and mayo?

"Oh." My tone sounds as pathetic as I feel. Glancing up, I find these two watching me. Riley's eyes are wide, open to the possibility of course, but Dylan bites her bottom lip. I know she's trying to keep from laughing because she was there the night of our hideous double date. Since then, besides her wedding, I've tried to keep any and all encounters with Zac Wright to the bare minimum. "Why?"

"Zac's mom is a great lawyer, in fact calling her great doesn't do her experience justice," Dylan says as she leans across to grab some crackers and cheese from the plate I'd put in the middle of the table.

"Justice. That's funny" Riley manages as she giggles. When Dylan shoots her a look, she rolls her eyes. "Leave me alone, I like a good pun."

It's my turn to hold back my smile. Ignoring us, Dylan pushes on. "She was asked to run for State Attorney General, but she turned it down. I'm sure I can talk to Zac and ask if he'll--"

"Nope." The word shoots from my mouth like an arrow. "Sorry, I don't mean to sound so cranky but Zac isn't the person I want helping me. Not now, not ever."

I can't ignore the look that passes between these two this time. I know they're my friends, and they only want to help, but right now I need them to understand this particular suggestion is the worst one ever.

"I can see you two looking at each other like that, I'm sitting right here." Standing up, I walk into the kitchen and pull three bottles of water out of the fridge, returning and handing them out. "Look, I appreciate the brain trust trying to help me out, but I think it's something I need to do on my own. I'm sure someone in my family knows a lawyer I can talk to, get some more advice."

"Okay, but the offer still stands." Dylan smiles at me and tilts her head to the side. "You two are like oil and water."

"He needs a sign hung around his neck that says 'Does not play well with others' and I mean that." Huffing, I sit back down on the couch beside her. "In fact, I'll even buy him the tee shirt if there is one."

"That bad, huh?" Riley says as she stands up, walks over to the hall table by my front door and grabs her purse. She pulls her phone out. "I could call him for you and ask."

"Please put your phone away. I'm fighting the urge to jump over there and tackle you."

"I'm joking!" She holds her phone up and shakes it in the air. "Not to change the subject, although I doubt you'll be sad I do, I'm going to call for some food to be delivered. My treat. What do you two feel like? Mexican, Thai, or pizza?"

"Pizza." Dylan and I say simultaneously, cracking us up.

"You're easy. I'll order two, be back in a sec."

Riley disappears into the back of my small home with the phone in her hand, and Dylan turns back to face me, her expression super serious.

"So, if you change your mind let me know. I'm happy to talk to Zac for you if you want."

"No, Dylan, I appreciate it but I mean it." Adamantly, I shake my head from side to side. "Let's not even bring it up again, if that's cool? At least not tonight. I need the escape of being here with you two and not thinking."

Dylan's eyes search mine, and it's not long until she nods her head once and relaxes in her seat again. "Deal. I'll drop it."

"Good. " Satisfied, I lean over and hug her before hopping up again. Spying the empty bottle of wine on the table, I swipe it and head to my walk-in pantry. "We'll need one more of these for the night, be right back."

It's times like this I appreciate the fact I can walk into this little pantry and close the door behind me. As the door shuts, I lean back against the wall and wipe the wet that hits my cheeks once I'm out of sight. There is no way I'm going to be the downer tonight.

As I gather my composure, I take some deep, slow breaths and look around at the small wine selection I have here. My eyes flick across the labels until I settle on one that's an old favorite of mine, plucking it off the shelf.

I will not ask Zac Wright for help, I don't care who his mother is or the fact he could very well help me right now. Honestly, I cannot stand that man. He's too much for me. Zac seems like the kind of guy who is a little slack, comes from privilege, and doesn't understand hard work. At least that's my take in the small window of time I've had with him. I do know that if we worked together, I'd want to get him fired.

No. I do not want Zac Wright's help. Ever. Even if he knows the judge who is hearing my case. No.

There's a squeal from the other side of the door and I hear Riley call my name. Closing my eyes, I steel myself. Here's hoping my issues, personal problems, and all of the weight I'm carrying on my shoulders doesn't come bursting forth like some kind of broken dam, because no. Not right now.

I take another breath while Dylan laughs hysterically at something Riley says.

Here's hoping.

Thank you so much for reading The Art of Falling in Love with Your Best Friend!

Want to know when Etta and Zac's story––*The Art of Dating Mr. Wright*––releases in August 2023? You can sign up for my newsletter here and stay up to date!

Looking for more content like bonus scenes, surprise chapters, and some of Reid's...whoops, I mean Andrew's columns for Culture Shock? Maybe you want to have *early access* to the next book BEFORE it's released?

Then join me on Ream, along with some of your fellow readers, and let's hang out there!

No matter where we end up, I know we'll have a blast together!

Anne xoxo

Also by Anne Kemp

Love in Lake Lorelei Series

Sweet RomComs sizzling with chemistry and bringing you all the feels. Get to know this small town, its locals and, most importantly, the Lake Lorelei Fire Department!

Sweet Summer Nights (Book 1)

Freya and Wyatt's story

The Sweet Spot (Book 2)

Ari and Carter's story

When Sparks Fly (Book 3)

Maisey and Jack's story

The Abby George Series

The Abby George books are closed-door, Chick lit comedies with a lil' sass, a touch of sarcasm, and some innuendo and language (especially from the salty captain!) but guaranteed to have you laughing out loud as you fall in love!

Rum Punch Regrets

Gotta Go To Come Back

Sugar City Secrets

Caribbean Romance Novella

Part of the Abby George world but can be read as a stand alone story.

This book is a sweet and clean closed door

romantic comedy.

Second Chance for Christmas

Stay up-to-date on new releases, get special bonus content, and special promotions when you sign up for

Anne's newsletter.

Acknowledgments

I'm honestly never sure where to start when I'm writing these, there are always so many amazing people to thank! I think I'll start with you, person reading this, because you're here reading my book and for that I am beyond grateful. I love escaping into these worlds and, since this is the first book in a new series, well...we're about to enter into a new one together, aren't we?

THANK YOU so much to the community who backs me through Bookstagram and BookTok! I've met so many amazing folks in both of these spaces over the last two years, and they all fill my heart full of joy! I'm a lucky, lucky lady.

My PA Sabrina is the woman behind the woman...she takes on tasks so I have space to get the writing done. I'm always grateful for you, S. Thank you.

To the Writer Frenz: You KNOW what y'all do for me! Thank you for the hand holding and encouragement to get my head back in the game. Everyone needs a posse full of golden hearts like yours!!

To my sister and my family in the USA...every. day. I. think. of. you.

Glen - I saved you for last because you still doubt I got Wordle in One. ;) I'll never be able to thank you enough for everything you do when I disappear to write. George and Charlie both say thank you, too, for walking them when I can't. We all love you!

To the readers, to the dreamers, to the impossibility believers: is there something you want to do, something you need to tick off your bucket list? Do it.

Life truly is short, go and do the thing!

Anne xoxo

About the Author

Anne Kemp is an author of romantic comedies, sweet contemporary romance, and chick lit.
She loves reading (and does it ridiculously fast, too!), gluten-free baking
(because everyone needs a hobby that makes them crazy), and finding time to binge-watch her favorite shows. She grew up in Maryland but made Los Angeles her home until she encountered her own real-life meet-cute at a friend's wedding where she ended up married to one of the groomsmen.
For real.

Anne now lives on the Kapiti Coast in New Zealand, and even though she was married at Mt. Doom, no...she doesn't have a Hobbit. However, she and her husband do have a terrier named George Clooney and a rescue pup named Charlie. When she's not writing, she's usually with them taking a long walk on the river by their home.

You can find Anne on her website www.annekemp.com or find her on social media.
She's on TikTok and Instagram as @annekempauthor and on Facebook and Twitter @missannekemp.

Made in United States
North Haven, CT
27 July 2024

55483862R00125